D0886788

MISSILE GAP

CHARLES STROSS

★ ★ ★

ILLUSTRATED BY J. K. POTTER

SUBTERRANEAN PRESS ★ 2006

Second Printing

Trade Hardcover Edition
ISBN 1-59606-058-1

Subterranean Press
PO Box 190106
Burton, MI 48519

Bomb scare

Gregor is feeding pigeons down in the park when the sirens go off.

A stoop-shouldered forty-something male in a dark suit, pale-skinned and thin, he pays no attention at first: the birds hold his attention. He stands at the side of a tarmac path, surrounded by damp grass that appears to have been sprayed with concrete dust, and digs into the outer pocket of his raincoat for a final handful of stale bread-crumbs. Filthy, soot-blackened city pigeons with malformed feet jostle with plump white-collared wood pigeons, pecking and lunging for morsels. Gregor doesn't smile. What to him is a handful of stale bread, is a deadly business for the birds: a matter of survival. The avian struggle for survival runs parallel to the human condition, he ponders. It's all a matter of limited resources and critical positioning. Of intervention by agencies beyond their bird-brained understanding, dropping treats for them to fight over. Then the air raid sirens start up.

The pigeons scatter for the treetops with a clatter of wings. Gregor straightens and looks round. It's not just one siren, and not just a test: a policeman is pedaling his bicycle along the path towards him, waving one-handed. "You there! Take cover!"

Gregor turns and presents his identity card. "Where is the nearest shelter?"

The constable points towards a public convenience thirty yards away. "The basement there. If you can't make it inside, you'll have to take cover behind the east wall—if you're caught in the open, just duck and cover in the nearest low spot. Now go!" The cop hops back on his black boneshaker and is off down the footpath before Gregor can frame a reply. Shaking his head, he walks towards the public toilet and goes inside.

It's early spring, a weekday morning, and the toilet attendant seems to be taking the emergency as a personal comment on the cleanliness of his porcelain. He jumps up and down agitatedly as he shoves Gregor down the spiral staircase into the shelter, like a short troll in a blue uniform stocking his larder. "Three minutes!" shouts the troll. "Hold fast in three minutes!" So many people in London are wearing uniforms these days, Gregor reflects; it's almost as if they believe that if they play their wartime role properly the ineffable will constrain itself to their expectations of a humanly comprehensible enemy.

A double-bang splits the air above the park and echoes down the stairwell. It'll be RAF or USAF interceptors outbound from the big fighter base near Hanworth. Gregor glances round: A couple of oafish gardeners sit on the wooden benches inside the concrete tunnel of the shelter, and a louche City type in a suit leans against the wall, irritably fiddling with an unlit cigarette and glaring at the NO SMOKING signs. "Bloody nuisance, eh?" he snarls in Gregor's direction.

Gregor composes his face in a thin smile. "I couldn't possibly comment," he says, his Hungarian accent betraying his status as a refugee. (Another sonic boom rattles the urinals, signaling the passage of yet more fighters.) The louche businessman will be his contact, Goldsmith. He glances at the shelter's counter. Its dial is twirling slowly, signaling the marked absence of radon and fallout. Time to make small-talk, verbal primate grooming: "Does it happen often?"

The corporate tough relaxes. He chuckles to himself. He'll have pegged Gregor as a visitor from stranger shores, the new NATO dominions overseas where they settled the latest wave of

refugees ejected by the communists. Taking in the copy of *The Telegraph* and the pattern of stripes on Gregor's tie he'll have realized what else Gregor is to him. "You should know, you took your time getting down here. Do you come here often to visit the front line, eh?"

"I am here in this bunker with you," Gregor shrugs. "There is no front line on a circular surface." He sits down on the bench opposite the businessman gingerly. "Cigarette?"

"Don't mind if I do." The businessman borrows Gregor's cigarette case with a flourish: the symbolic peace-offering accepted, they sit in silence for a couple of minutes, waiting to find out if it's the curtain call for world war four, or just a trailer.

A different note drifts down the staircase, the warbling tone that indicates the all-clear these days. The Soviet bombers have turned for home, the ragged lion's stumpy tail tickled yet again. The toilet troll dashes down the staircase and windmills his arms at them: "No smoking in the nuclear bunker!" he screams. "*Get out!* Out, I say!"

Gregor walks back into Regent's Park, to finish disposing of his stale bread-crumbs and ferry the contents of his cigarette case back to the office. The businessman doesn't know it yet, but he's going to be arrested, and his English nationalist/neutralist cabal interned: meanwhile, Gregor is being recalled to Washington DC. This is his last visit, at least on this particular assignment. There are thin times ahead for the wood pigeons.

Voyage

It's a moonless night and the huge reddened whirlpool of the Milky Way lies below the horizon. With only the reddish-white pinprick glare of Lucifer for illumination, it's too dark to read a newspaper.

Maddy is old enough to remember a time when night was something else: when darkness stalked the heavens, the Milky Way a faded tatter spun across half the sky. A time when ominous Soviet spheres bleeped and hummed their way across a horizon that curved, when geometry was dominated by pi, astronomy made sense, and serious men with horn-rimmed glasses and German accents were going to the moon. October 2, 1962: that's when it all changed. That's when life stopped making sense. (Of course it first stopped making sense a few days earlier, with the U-2 flights over the concrete emplacements in Cuba, but there was a difference between the lunacy of brinksmanship—Khrushchev's shoe banging on the table at the UN as he shouted "we will bury you!"—and the flat earth daydream that followed, shattering history and plunging them all into this nightmare of revisionist geography.)

But back to the here-and-now: she's sitting on the deck of an elderly ocean liner on her way from somewhere to nowhere, and she's annoyed because Bob is getting drunk with the F-deck boys again and eating into their precious grubstake. It's too dark to read the ship's daily news sheet (mimeographed blurry headlines from a world already fading into the ship's wake), it'll be at least two weeks before their next landfall (a refueling depot somewhere in what the National Oceanic and Atmospheric Administration surveyors—in a fit of uncharacteristic wit—named the Nether Ocean), and she's half out of her skull with boredom.

When they signed up for the Emigration Board tickets Bob had joked: "A six month cruise? After a vacation like that we'll be happy to get back to work!"—but somehow the sheer immensity of it all didn't sink in until the fourth week out of sight of land. In those four weeks they'd crawled an expanse of ocean wider than the Pacific, pausing to refuel twice from huge rust-colored barges: and still they were only a sixth of the way to Continent F-204, New Iowa, immersed like the ultimate nonsequitur in the ocean that replaced the world's horizons on October 2, 1962. Two weeks later they passed The Radiators. The Radiators thrust from the oceanic depths to the stratosphere, Everest-high black fins finger-combing the watery currents. Beyond them the tropical heat of the Pacific gave way to the subarctic chill of the Nether Ocean. Sailing between them, the ship was reduced to the proportions of a cockroach crawling along a canyon between skyscrapers. Maddy had taken one look at these guardians of the interplanetary ocean, shuddered, and retreated into their cramped room for the two days it took to sail out from between the slabs.

Bob kept going on about how materials scientists from NOAA and the National Institutes were still trying to understand what they were made of, until Maddy snapped at him. He didn't seem to understand that they were the bars on a prison cell. He seemed to see a waterway as wide as the English Channel, and a gateway to the future: but Maddy saw them as a sign that her old life was over.

If only Bob and her father hadn't argued; or if Mum hadn't tried to pick a fight with her over Bob—

Maddy leans on the railing and sighs, and a moment later nearly jumps out of her skin as a strange man clears his throat behind her.

"Excuse me, I didn't mean to disturb you."

"That's alright," Maddy replies, irritated and trying to conceal it. "I was just going in."

"A shame: it's a beautiful night," says the stranger. He turns and puts down a large briefcase next to the railing, fiddling with the latches. "Not a cloud in sight, just right for stargazing." She focuses on him, seeing short hair, small paunch, and a worried thirty-something face. He doesn't look back, being preoccupied with something that resembles a photographer's tripod.

"Is that a telescope?" she asks, eyeing the stubby cylindrical gadget in his case.

"Yes." An awkward pause. "Name's John Martin. Yourself?"

"Maddy Holbright." Something about his diffident manner puts her at ease. "Are you settling? I haven't seen you around."

He straightens up and tightens joints on the tripod's legs, screwing them into place. "I'm not a settler, I'm a researcher. Five years, all expenses paid, to go and explore a new continent." He carefully lifts the telescope body up and lowers it onto the platform, then begins tightening screws. "And I'm supposed to point this thing at the sky and make regular observations. I'm actually an entomologist, but there are so many things to do that they want me to be a jack of all trades, I guess."

"So they've got you to carry a telescope, huh? I don't think I've ever met an entomologist before."

"A bug-hunter with a telescope," he agrees: "kind of unexpected."

Intrigued, Maddy watches as he screws the viewfinder into place then pulls out a notebook and jots something down. "What are you looking at?"

He shrugs. "There's a good view of S-Doradus from here," he says. "You know, Satan? And his two little angels."

Maddy glances up at the violent pinprick of light, then looks away before it can burn her eyes. It's a star, but bright enough to cast shadows from half a light year's distance. "The disks?"

"Them." There's a camera body in his bag, a chunky old Bronica from back before the Soviets swallowed Switzerland and Germany whole. He carefully screws it onto the telescope's viewfinder. "The Institute wants me to take a series of photographs of them—nothing fancy, just the best this eight-inch reflector can do—over six months. Plot the ship's position on a map. There's a bigger telescope in the hold, for when I arrive, and they're talking about sending a real astronomer one of these days, but in the meantime they want photographs from sixty thousand miles out across the disk. For parallax, so they can work out how fast the disks are moving."

"Disks." They seem like distant abstractions to her, but John's enthusiasm is hard to ignore. "Do you suppose they're like, uh, here?" She doesn't say like *Earth*—everybody knows this isn't Earth any more. Not the way it used to be.

"Maybe." He busies himself for a minute with a chunky film cartridge. "They've got oxygen in their atmospheres, we know that. And they're big enough. But they're most of a light year away—far closer than the stars, but still too far for telescopes."

"Or moon rockets," she says, slightly wistfully. "Or sputniks."

"If those things worked any more." The film is in: he leans over the scope and brings it round to bear on the first of the disks, a couple of degrees off from Satan. (The disks are invisible to the naked eye; it takes a telescope to see their reflected light.) He glances up at her. "Do you remember the moon?"

Maddy shrugs. "I was just a kid when it happened. But I saw the moon, some nights. During the day, too."

He nods. "Not like some of the kids these days. Tell them we used to live on a big spinning sphere and they look at you like you're mad."

"What do they think the speed of the disks will tell them?" She asks.

"Whether they're all as massive as this one. What they could be made of. What that tells us about who it was that made them." He shrugs. "Don't ask me, I'm just a bug-hunter. This stuff is *big*, bigger than bugs." He chuckles. "It's a new world out here."

She nods very seriously, then actually sees him for the first time: "I guess it is."

Boldly Go

"So tell me, comrade colonel, how did it really feel?"

The comrade colonel laughs uneasily. He's forty-three and still slim and boyish-looking, but carries a quiet melancholy around with him like his own personal storm cloud. "I was very busy all the time," he says with a self-deprecating little shrug. "I didn't have time to pay attention to myself. One orbit, it only lasted ninety minutes, what did you expect? If you really want to know, Gherman's the man to ask. He had more time."

"Time." His interrogator sighs and leans his chair back on two legs. It's a horribly old, rather precious Queen Anne original, a gift to some Tsar or other many years before the October revolution. "What a joke. Ninety minutes, two days, that's all we got before they changed the rules on us."

"'They,' comrade chairman?" The colonel looked puzzled.

"Whoever." The chairman's vague wave takes in half the horizon of the richly paneled Kremlin office. "What a joke. Whoever they were, at least they saved us from a pasting in Cuba because of that louse Nikita." He pauses for a moment, then toys with the wine glass that sits, half-empty, before him. The colonel has a glass too, but his is full of grape juice, out of consideration for his past difficulties. "The 'whoever' I speak of are of course the brother socialists from the stars who brought us here." He grins humorlessly, face creasing like the muzzle of a shark that smells blood in the water.

"Brother socialists." The colonel smiles hesitantly, wondering if it's a joke, and if so, whether he's allowed to share it. He's still unsure why he's being interviewed by the premier—in his private office, at that. "Do we know anything of them, sir? That is, am I supposed to—"

"Never mind." Aleksey sniffs, dismissing the colonel's worries. "Yes, you're cleared to know everything on this topic. The trouble is there is nothing to know, and this troubles me, Yuri Alexeyevich. We infer purpose, the engine of a greater history at work—but the dialectic is silent on this matter. I have consulted the experts, asked them to read the chicken entrails, but none of them can do anything other than parrot pre-event dogma: 'any species advanced enough to do to us what happened that day must of course have evolved true Communism, comrade premier! Look what they did for us! (That was Shchlovskii, by the way.) And yes, I look and I see six cities that nobody can live in, spaceships that refuse to stick to the sky, and a landscape that Sakharov and that bunch of double-domes are at a loss to explain. There are fucking miracles and wonders and portents in the sky, like a galaxy we were supposed to be part of that is now a million years too old and shows extensive signs of construction. There's no room for miracles and wonders in our rational world, and it's giving the comrade general secretary, Yuri, the *comrade general secretary,* stomach ulcers; did you know that?"

The colonel sits up straight, anticipating the punch line: it's a well-known fact throughout the USSR that when Brezhnev says 'frog,' the premier croaks. And here he is in the premier's office, watching that very man, Aleksey Kosygin, chairman of the Council of Ministers, third most powerful man in the Soviet Union, taking a deep breath.

"Yuri Alexeyevich, I have brought you here today because I want you to help set Leonid Illich's stomach at rest. You're an aviator and a hero of the Soviet Union, and more importantly you're smart enough to do the job and young enough to see it through, not like the old farts cluttering up Stavka. (It's going to take most of a lifetime to sort out, you mark my words.) You're also, you will pardon the bluntness, about as much use as a fifth wheel in your current posting right now: we have to face facts, and the sad reality is that none of Korolev's birds will ever fly again, not even with the atomic bomb pusher-thing they've been working on." Kosygin sighs and shuffles upright in his chair. "There is simply no point in maintaining the Cosmonaut Training Centre. A decree has been drafted and will be approved next week: the manned rocket program is going to be wound up and the cosmonaut corps reassigned to other duties."

The colonel flinches. "Is that absolutely necessary, comrade chairman?"

Kosygin drains his wine glass, decides to ignore the implied criticism. "We don't have the resources to waste. But, Yuri Alexeyevich, all that training is not lost." He grins wolfishly. "I have new worlds for you to explore, and a new ship for you to do it in."

"A new ship." The colonel nods then does a double take, punch-drunk. "A ship?"

"Well, it isn't a fucking horse," says Kosygin. He slides a big glossy photograph across his blotter towards the colonel. "Times have moved on." The colonel blinks in confusion as he tries to make sense of the thing at the centre of the photograph. The premier watches his face, secretly amused: confusion is *everybody's* first reaction to the thing in the photograph.

"I'm not sure I understand, sir—"

"It's quite simple: you trained to explore new worlds. You can't, not using the rockets. The rockets won't ever make orbit. I've had astronomers having nervous breakdowns trying to explain why, but the all agree on the key point: rockets won't do it for us here. Something wrong with the gravity, they say it even crushes falling starlight." The chairman taps a fat finger on the photograph. "But you can do it using *this*. We invented it and the bloody Americans didn't. It's called an ekranoplan, and you rocket boys are going to stop being grounded cosmonauts and learn how to fly it. What do you think, colonel Gagarin?"

The colonel whistles tunelessly through his teeth: he's finally worked out the scale. It looks like a flying boat with clipped wings, jet engines clustered by the sides of its cockpit—but no flying boat ever carried a runway with a brace of MiG-21s on its back. "It's bigger than a cruiser! Is it nuclear powered?"

"Of course." The chairman's grin slips. "It cost as much as those moon rockets of Sergei's, *colonel-general*. Try not to drop it."

Gagarin glances up, surprise and awe visible on his face. "Sir, I'm honored, but—"

"Don't be." The chairman cuts him off. "The promotion was coming your way anyway. The posting that comes with it will earn you as much honor as that first orbit. A second chance at space, if you like. But you can't fail: the cost is unthinkable. It's not your skin that will pay the toll, it's our entire rationalist civilization." Kosygin leans forward intently.

"Somewhere out there are beings so advanced that they skinned the earth like a grape and plated it onto this disk—or worse, copied us all right down to the atomic level and duplicated us like one of those American Xerox machines. It's not just us, though. You are aware of the other continents in the oceans. We think some of them may be inhabited, too—nothing else makes sense. Your task is to take the *Sergei Korolev,* the first ship of its class, on an historic five-year cruise. You will boldly go where no Soviet man has gone before, explore new worlds and look for new peoples, and to establish fraternal socialist relations with them. But your primary objective is to discover who built this giant mousetrap of a world, and why they brought us to it, and to report back to us—*before* the Americans find out."

Committee process

The cherry trees are in bloom in Washington DC, and Gregor perspires in the summer heat. He has grown used to the relative cool of London and this unaccustomed change of climate has disoriented him. Jet lag is a thing of the past—a small mercy—but there are still adjustments to make. Because the disk is flat, the daylight source—polar flares from an accretion disk inside the axial hole, the scientists call it, which signifies nothing to most people—grows and shrinks the same wherever you stand.

There's a concrete sixties-vintage office block with a conference suite furnished in burnt umber and orange, chromed chairs and Kandinsky prints on the walls: all very seventies. Gregor waits outside the suite until the buzzer sounds and the receptionist looks up from behind her IBM typewriter and says, "You can go in now, they're expecting you."

Gregor goes in. It's an occupational hazard, but by no means the worst, in his line of work.

"Have a seat." It's Seth Brundle, Gregor's divisional head—a grey-looking functionary, more adept at office back-stabbing than field-expedient assassinations. His cover, like Gregor's, is an innocuous-sounding post in the Office of Technology Assessment. In fact, both he and Gregor work for a different government agency, although the notional task is the same: identify technological threats and stamp on them before they emerge.

Brundle is not alone in the room. He proceeds with the introductions: "Greg Samsa is our London station chief and specialist in scientific intelligence. Greg, this is Marcus." The bald, thin-faced German in the smart suit bobs his head and smiles behind his horn-rimmed glasses. "Civilian consultant." Gregor mistrusts him on sight. Marcus is a defector—a former Stasi spook, from back before the Brezhnev purges of the mid-sixties. Which puts an interesting complexion on this meeting.

"Murray Fox, from Langley."

"Hi," says Gregor, wondering just what kind of insane political critical mass Stone is trying to assemble: Langley and Brundle's parent outfit aren't even on speaking terms, to say the least.

"And another civilian specialist, Dr. Sagan." Greg nods at the doctor, a thin guy with sparkling brown eyes and hippyish long hair. "Greg's got something to tell us in person," says Brundle. "Something very interesting he picked up in London. No sources please, Greg."

"No sources," Gregor echoes. He pulls out a chair and sits down. Now he's here he supposes he'll just have to play the role Brundle assigned to him in the confidential briefing he read on the long flight home. "We have word from an unimpeachable HUMINT resource that the Russians have—" he coughs into his fist. "Excuse me." He glances at Brundle. "Okay to talk about COLLECTION RUBY?"

"They're all cleared," Brundle says dryly. "That's why it says 'joint committee' on the letterhead."

"I see. My invitation was somewhat terse." Gregor stifles a sigh that seems to say, *all I get is a most urgent recall; how am I meant to know what's going on and who knows what?* "So why are we here?"

"Think of it as another collective analysis board," says Fox, the man from the CIA. He doesn't look enthused.

"We're here to find out what's going on, with the benefit of some intelligence resources from the other side of the curtain."

Doctor Sagan, who has been listening silently with his head cocked to one side like a very intelligent blackbird, raises an eyebrow.

"Yes?" asks Brundle.

"I, uh, would you mind explaining that to me? I haven't been on one of these committees before."

No indeed, thinks Gregor. It's a miracle Sagan ever passed his political vetting: he's too friendly by far with some of those Russian astronomer guys who are clearly under the thumb of the KGB's First Department. And he's expressed doubts—muted, of course—about the thrust of current foreign policy, which is a serious no-no under the McNamara administration.

"A CAB is a joint committee feeding into the Central Office of Information's external bureaux on behalf of a blue-ribbon panel of experts assembled from the intelligence community," Gregor recites in a bored tone of voice. "Stripped of the bullshit, we're a board of wise men who're meant to rise above narrow bureaucratic lines of engagement and prepare a report for the Office of Technology Assessment to pass on to the Director of Central Intelligence. It's not meant to reflect the agenda of any one department, but to be a Delphi board synergizing our lateralities. Set up after the Cuban fiasco to make sure that we never again get backed into that kind of corner by accidental groupthink. One of the rules of the CAB process is that it has to include at least one dissident: unlike the commies we know we're not perfect." Gregor glances pointedly at Fox, who has the good sense to stay silent.

"Oh, I see," Sagan says hesitantly. With more force: "so that's why I'm here? Is that the only reason you've dragged me away from Cornell?"

"Of course not, Doctor," oozes Brundle, casting Gregor a dirty look. The East German defector, Wolff, maintains a smug silence: *I are above all this.* "We're here to come up with policy recommendations for dealing with the bigger picture. The *much* bigger picture."

"The Builders," says Fox. "We're here to determine what our options look like if and when they show up, and to make recommendations about the appropriate course of action. Your background in, uh, SETI recommended you."

Sagan looks at him in disbelief. "I'd have thought that was obvious," he says.

"Eh?"

"We won't have any choice," the young professor explains with a wry smile. "Does a termite mound negotiate with a nuclear superpower?"

Brundle leans forward. "That's rather a radical position, isn't it? Surely there'll be some room for maneuver? We know this is an artificial construct, but presumably the builders are still living people. Even if they've got green skin and six eyes."

"Oh. My. God." Sagan leans forward, his face in his hands. After a moment Gregor realizes that he's laughing.

"Excuse me." Gregor glances round. It's the German defector, Wolff, or whatever he's called. "Herr Professor, would you care to explain what you find so funny?"

After a moment Sagan leans back, looks at the ceiling, and sighs. "Imagine a single, a forty-five RPM record with a centre hole punched out. The inner hole is half an astronomical unit—forty-six million miles—in radius. The outer edge is of unknown radius, but probably about two and a half AUs—two hundred and forty five million miles. The disk's thickness is unknown—seismic waves are reflected off a mirror-like rigid layer eight hundred miles down—but we can estimate it at eight thousand miles, if its density averages out at the same as Earth's. Surface gravity is the same as our original planet, and since we've been transplanted here and survived we have learned that it's a remarkably hospitable environment for our kind of life; only on the large scale does it seem different."

The astronomer sits up. "Do any of you gentlemen have any idea just how preposterously powerful whoever built this structure is?"

"How do you mean, preposterously powerful?" asks Brundle, looking more interested than annoyed.

"A colleague of mine, Dan Alderson, did the first analysis. I think you might have done better to pull him in, frankly. Anyway, let me itemise: item number one is escape velocity." Sagan holds up a bony finger. "Gravity on a disk does not diminish in accordance with the inverse square law, the way it does on a spherical object like the planet we came from. We have roughly earthlike gravity, but to escape, or to reach orbit, takes tremendously more speed. Roughly two hundred times more, in fact. Rockets that from Earth could reach the moon just fall out of the sky after running out of fuel. Next item:" another finger. "The area and mass of the disk. If it's double-sided it has a surface area equal to billions and billions of Earths. We're stuck in the middle of an ocean full of alien continents, but we have no guarantee that this hospitable environment is anything other than a tiny oasis in a world of strangeness."

The astronomer pauses to pour himself a glass of water, then glances round the table. "To put it in perspective, gentlemen, this world is so big that, if one in every hundred stars had an earth-like planet, this single structure could support the population of our *entire home galaxy.* As for the mass—this structure is as massive as fifty thousand suns. It is, quite bluntly, impossible: as-yet unknown physical forces must be at work to keep it from rapidly collapsing in on itself and creating a black hole. The repulsive force, whatever it is, is strong enough to hold the weight of fifty thousand suns: think about that for a moment, gentlemen."

At that point Sagan looks around and notices the blank stares. He chuckles ruefully.

"What I mean to say is, this structure is not permitted by the laws of physics as we understand them. Because it clearly *does* exist, we can draw some conclusions, starting with the fact that our understanding of physics is incomplete. Well, that isn't news: we know we don't have a unified theory of everything. Einstein spent thirty years looking for one, and didn't come up with it. But, secondly." He looks tired for a moment, aged beyond his years. "We used to think that any extraterrestrial beings we might communicate with would be fundamentally comprehensible: folks like us, albeit with better technology. I think that's the frame of mind you're still working in. Back in sixty-one we had a brainstorming session at a conference, trying to work out just how big an engineering project a spacefaring civilization might come up with. Freeman Dyson, from Princeton, came up with about the biggest thing any of us could imagine: something that required us to imagine dismantling Jupiter and turning it into habitable real estate.

"This disk is about a hundred million times bigger than Dyson's sphere. And that's before we take into account the time factor."

"Time?" Echoes Fox from Langley, sounding confused.

"Time." Sagan smiles in a vaguely disconnected way. "We're nowhere near our original galactic neighborhood and whoever moved us here, they didn't bend the laws of physics far enough to violate the speed limit. It takes light about 160,000 years to cross the distance between where we used to live, and our new stellar neighborhood, the Lesser Magellanic Cloud. Which we have fixed, incidentally, by measuring the distance to known Cepheid variables, once we were able to take into account the measurable red shift of infalling light and the fact that some of them were changing frequency slowly and seem to have changed rather a lot. Our best estimate is eight hundred thousand years, plus or minus two hundred thousand. That's about four times as long as our species has *existed,* gentlemen. We're fossils, an archaeology experiment or something. Our relevance to our abductors is not as equals, but as subjects in some kind of vast experiment. And what the purpose of the experiment is, I can't tell you. I've got some guesses, but…"

Sagan shrugs, then lapses into silence. Gregor catches Brundle's eye and Brundle shakes his head, very slightly. *Don't spill the beans.* Gregor nods. Sagan may realize he's in a room with a CIA spook and an East German defector, but he doesn't need to know about the Alienation Service yet.

"Well that's as may be," says Fox, dropping words like stones into the hollow silence at the table. "But it begs the question, what are we going to tell the DCI?"

"I suggest," says Gregor, "that we start by reviewing COLLECTION RUBY." He nods at Sagan. "Then, maybe when we're all up to speed on *that*, we'll have a better idea of whether there's anything useful we can tell the DCI."

Cannon-Fodder

Madeleine and Robert Holbright are among the last of the immigrants to disembark on the new world. As she glances back at the brilliant white side of the liner, the horizon seems to roll around her head, settling into a strange new stasis that feels unnatural after almost six months at sea.

New Iowa isn't flat and it isn't new: rampart cliffs loom to either side of the unnaturally deep harbor (gouged out of bedrock courtesy of General Atomics). A cog-driven funicular railway hauls Maddy and Robert and their four shipping trunks up the thousand-foot climb to the plateau and the port city of Fort Eisenhower—and then to the arrival and orientation camp.

Maddy is quiet and withdrawn, but Bob, oblivious, natters constantly about opportunities and jobs and grabbing a plot of land to build a house on. "It's the new world," he says at one point: "why aren't you excited?"

"The new world," Maddy echoes, biting back the urge to say something cutting. She looks out the window as the train climbs the cliff-face and brings them into sight of the city. *City* is the wrong word: it implies solidity, permanence. Fort Eisenhower is less than five years old, a leukaemic gash inflicted on the landscape by the Corps of Engineers. The tallest building is the governor's mansion, at three stories. Architecturally the town is all Wild West meets the Radar Age, raw pine houses contrasting with big grey concrete boxes full of seaward-pointing Patriot missiles to deter the inevitable encroachment of the communist hordes. "It's so *flat.*"

"The nearest hills are two hundred miles away, past the coastal plain—didn't you read the map?"

She ignores his little dig as the train squeals and clanks up the side of the cliff. It wheezes asthmatically to a stop besides a wooden platform, and expires in a belch of saturated steam. An hour later they're weary and sweated-up in the lobby of an unprepossessing barrack-hall made of plywood. There's a large hall and a row of tables and a bunch of bored-looking colonial service types, and people are walking from one position to another with bundles of papers, answering questions in low voices and receiving official stamps. The would-be colonists mill around like disturbed livestock among the piles of luggage at the back of the room. Maddy and Robert queue uneasy in the damp afternoon heat, overhearing snippets of conversation. "Country of origin? Educational qualifications? Yes, but what was your last job?" Religion and race—almost a quarter of the people in the hall are refugees from India or Pakistan or somewhere lost to the mysterious east forever—seem to obsess the officials. "Robert?" she whispers.

"It'll be alright," he says with false certainty. Taking after his dad already, trying to pretend he's the solid family man. Her sidelong glance at him steals any residual confidence. Then it's their turn.

"Names, passports, country of origin?" The guy with the moustache is brusque and bored, irritated by the heat.

Robert smiles at him. "Robert and Madeleine Holbright, from Canada?" He offers their passports.

"Uh-huh." The official gives the documents a very American going-over. "What schooling have you done? What was your last job?"

"I've, uh, I was working part-time in a garage. On my way through college—I was final year at Toronto, studying structural engineering, but I haven't sat the finals. Maddy—Maddy's a qualified paramedic."

The officer fixes her with a stare. "Worked at it?"

"What? Uh, no—I'm freshly qualified." His abrupt questioning flusters her.

"Huh." He makes a cryptic notation against their names on a long list, a list that spills over the edge of his desk and trails towards the rough floor. "Next." He hands the passports back, and a couple of cards, and points them along to the row of desks.

Someone is already stepping up behind them when Maddy manages to read the tickets. Hers says TRAINEE NURSE. Robert is staring at his and saying "no, this is wrong."

"What is it, Bob?" She looks over his shoulder as someone jostles him sideways. His card reads LABORER (unskilled); but she doesn't have time to read the rest.

Captain's Log

Yuri Gagarin kicks his shoes off, loosens his tie, and leans back in his chair. "It's hotter than fucking Cuba!" he complains.

"You visited Cuba, didn't you, boss?" His companion, still standing, pours a glass of iced tea and passes it to the young colonel-general before drawing one for himself.

"Yeah, thanks Misha." The former first cosmonaut smiles tiredly. "Back before the invasion. Have a seat."

Misha Gorodin is the only man on the ship who doesn't have to give a shit whether the captain offers him a seat, but he's grateful all the same: a little respect goes a long way, and Gagarin's sunny disposition and friendly attitude is a far cry from some of the fuckheads Misha's been stuck with in the past. There's a class of officer who thinks that because you're a *zampolit* you're somehow below them, but Yuri doesn't do that: in some ways he's the ideal New Soviet Man, progress personified. Which makes life a lot easier, because Yuri is one of the very few naval commanders who doesn't have to give a shit what his political officer thinks, and life would be an awful lot stickier without that grease of respect to make the wheels go round. Mind you, Yuri is also commander of the only naval warship operated by the Cosmonaut Corps, which is a branch of the Strategic Rocket Forces, another howling exception to the usual military protocol. Somehow this posting seems to be breaking all the rules…

"What was it like, boss?"

"Hot as hell. Humid, like this. Beautiful women but lots of dark-skinned comrades who didn't bathe often enough—all very jolly, but you couldn't help looking out to sea, over your shoulder. You know there was an American base there, even then? Guantanamo. They don't have the base now, but they've got *all* the rubble." For a moment Gagarin looks morose. "Bastards."

"The Americans."

"Yes. Shitting on a small defenseless island like that, just because they couldn't get to us any more. You remember when they had to hand out iodine tablets to all the kids? That wasn't Leningrad or Gorky, the fallout plume: it was Havana. I don't think they wanted to admit just how bad it was."

Misha sips his tea. "We had a lucky escape." Morale be damned, it's acceptable to admit at least that much in front of the CO, in private. Misha's seen some of the KGB reports on the US nuclear capabilities back then, and his blood runs cold; while Nikita had been wildly bluffing about the Rodina's nuclear defenses, the Americans had been hiding the true scale of their own arsenal. From themselves as much as the rest of the world.

"Yes. Things were going to the devil back then, no question: if we hadn't woken up over here, who knows what would have happened? They out-gunned us back then. I don't think they realized." Gagarin's dark expression lifts: he glances out of the open porthole—the only one in a private cabin that opens—and smiles. "This isn't Cuba, though." The headland rising above the bay tells him that much: no tropical island on earth supported such weird vegetation. Or such ruins.

"Indeed not. But, what about the ruins?" asks Misha, putting his tea glass down on the map table.

"Yes." Gagarin leans forward: "I was meaning to talk to you about that. Exploration is certainly in line with our orders, but we are a trifle short of trained archaeologists, aren't we? Let's see: we're four hundred and seventy thousand kilometers from home, six major climactic zones, five continents—it'll be a long time before we get any settlers out here, won't it?" He pauses delicately. "Even if the rumors about reform of the penal system are true."

"It is certainly a dilemma," Misha agrees amiably, deliberately ignoring the skipper's last comment. "But we can take some time over it. There's nobody out here, at least not within range of yesterday's reconnaissance flight. I'll vouch for lieutenant Chekhov's soundness: he has a solid attitude, that one."

"I don't see how we can leave without examining the ruins, but we've got limited resources and in any case I don't want to do anything that might get the Academy to slap our wrists. No digging for treasure until the egg-heads get here." Gagarin hums tunelessly for a moment, then slaps his hand on his thigh: "I think we'll shoot some film for the comrade general secretary's birthday party. First we'll secure a perimeter around the beach, give those damned spetsnaz a chance to earn all the vodka they've been drinking. Then you and I, we can take Primary Science Party Two into the nearest ruins with lights and cameras. Make a visual record, leave the double-domes back in Moscow to figure out what we're looking at and whether it's worth coming back later with a bunch of archaeologists. What do you say, Misha?"

"I say that's entirely logical, comrade general," says the political officer, nodding to himself.

"That's so ordered, then. We'll play it safe, though. Just because we haven't seen any active settlement patterns, doesn't mean there're no aborigines lurking in the forest."

"Like that last bunch of lizards." Misha frowns. "Little purple bastards!"

"We'll make good communists out of them eventually," Yuri insists. "A toast! To making good communists out of little purple lizard-bastards with blowpipes who shoot political officers in the arse!"

Gagarin grins wickedly and Gorodin knows when he's being wound up on purpose and summons a twinkle to his eye as he raises his glass: "And to poisons that don't work on human beings."

Discography

Warning:

The following briefing film is classified COLLECTION RUBY. If you do not possess both COLLECTION and RUBY clearances, leave the auditorium and report to the screening security officer immediately. Disclosure to unauthorized personnel is a federal offense punishable by a fine of up to ten thousand dollars and/or imprisonment for up to twenty years. You have thirty seconds to clear the auditorium and report to the screening security officer.

Voice-over:

Ocean—the final frontier. For twelve years, since the momentous day when we discovered that we had been removed to this planar world, we have been confronted by the immensity of an ocean that goes on as far as we can see. Confronted also by the prospect of the spread of Communism to uncharted new continents, we have committed ourselves to a strategy of exploration and containment.

Film clip:

An Atlas rocket on the launch pad rises slowly, flames jetting from its tail: it surges past the gantry and disappears into the sky.

Cut to:

A camera mounted in the nose, pointing back along the flank of the rocket. The ground falls behind, blurring into blue distance.

Slowly, the sky behind the rocket is turning black: but the land still occupies much of the fisheye view. The first stage engine ring tumbles away, leaving the core engine burning with a pale blue flame: now the outline of the California coastline is recognizable. North America shrinks visibly: eventually another, strange outline swims into view, like a cipher in an alien script. The booster burns out and falls behind, and the tumbling camera catches sunlight glinting off the upper-stage Centaur rocket as its engine ignites, thrusting it higher and faster.

Voice-over:

We cannot escape.

Cut to:

A meteor streaking across the empty blue bowl of the sky; slowing, deploying parachutes.

Voice-over:

In 1962, this rocket would have blasted a two-ton payload all the way into outer space. That was when we lived on a planet that was an oblate sphere. Life on a dinner-plate seems to be different: while the gravitational attraction anywhere on the surface is a constant, we can't get away from it. In fact, anything we fire straight up will come back down again. Not even a nuclear rocket can escape: according to JPL scientist Dan Alderson, escape from a Magellanic disk would require a speed of over one thousand six hundred miles per second. That is because this disk masses many times more than a star—in fact, it has a mass fifty thousand times greater than our own sun.

What stops it collapsing into a sphere? Nobody knows. Physicists speculate that a fifth force that drove the early expansion of the universe—they call it 'quintessence'—has been harnessed by the makers of the disk. But the blunt truth is, nobody knows for sure. Nor do we understand how we came here—how, in the blink of an eye, something beyond our comprehension peeled the earth's continents and oceans like a grape and plated them across this alien disk.

Cut to:

A map. The continents of earth are laid out—Americas at one side, Europe and Asia and Africa to their east. Beyond the Indonesian island chain Australia and New Zealand hang lonely on the edge of an abyss of ocean.

The map pans right: strange new continents swim into view, ragged-edged and huge. A few of them are larger than Asia and Africa combined; most of them are smaller.

Voice-over:

Geopolitics was changed forever by the Move. While the surface topography of our continents was largely preserved, wedges of foreign material were introduced below the Mohorovicik discontinuity—below the crust—and in the deep ocean floor, to act as spacers. The distances between points separated by deep ocean were, of necessity, changed, and not in our geopolitical favor. While the tactical balance of power after the Move was much as it had been before, the great circle flight paths our strategic missiles were designed for—over the polar ice cap and down into the Communist empire—were distorted and stretched, placing the enemy targets outside their range. Meanwhile, although our manned bombers could still reach Moscow with in-flight refueling, the changed map would have forced them to traverse thousands of miles of hostile airspace en route. The Move rendered most of our strategic preparations useless. If the British had been willing to stand firm, we might have prevailed—but in retrospect, what went for us also went for the Soviets, and it is hard to condemn the British for being unwilling to take the full force of the inevitable Soviet bombardment alone.

In retrospect the only reason this was not a complete disaster for us is that the Soviets were caught in the same disarray as ourselves. But the specter of Communism now dominates western Europe: the supposedly independent nations of the European Union are as much in thrall to Moscow as the client states of the Warsaw Pact. Only the on-going British State of Emergency offers us any residual geopolitical traction on the red continent, and in the long term we must anticipate that the British, too, will be driven to reach an accommodation with the Soviet Union.

Cut to:

A silvery delta-winged aircraft in flight. Stub wings, pointed nose, and a shortage of windows proclaim it to be an unmanned drone: a single large engine in its tail thrusts it along, exhaust nozzle glowing cherry-red. Trackless wastes unwind below it as the viewpoint—a chase plane—carefully climbs over the drone to capture a clear view of the upper fuselage.

Voice-over:

The disk is vast—so huge that it defies sanity. Some estimates give it the surface area of more than a billion earths. Exploration by conventional means is futile: hence the deployment of the NP-101 Persephone drone, here seen making a proving flight over land mass F-42. The NP-101 is a reconnaissance derivative of the nuclear-powered D-SLAM Pluto missile that forms the backbone of our post-Move deterrent force. It is slower than a strategic D-SLAM, but much more reliable: while D-SLAM is designed for a quick, fiery dash into Soviet territory, the NP-101 is designed to fly long duration missions that map entire continents. On a typical deployment the NP-101 flies outward at thrice the speed of sound for nearly a month: traveling fifty thousand miles a day, it penetrates a million miles into the unknown before it turns and flies homeward. Its huge mapping cameras record two images every thousand seconds, and its sophisticated digital computer records a variety of data from its sensor suite, allowing us to build up a picture of parts of the disk that our ships would take years or decades to reach. With resolution down to the level of a single nautical mile, the NP-101 program has been a resounding success, allowing us to map whole new worlds that it would take us years to visit in person.

At the end of its mission, the NP-101 drops its final film capsule and flies out into the middle of an uninhabited ocean, to ditch its spent nuclear reactor safely far from home.

Cut to:

A bull's-eye diagram. The centre is a black circle with a star at its heart; around it is a circular platter, of roughly the same proportions as a 45 rpm single.

Voice over:

A rough map of the disk. Here is the area we have explored to date, using the NP-101 program.

(A dot little larger than a sand grain lights up on the face of the single.)

That dot of light is a million kilometers in radius—five times the distance that used to separate our old Earth from its moon. (To cross the radius of the disk, an NP-101 would have to fly at Mach Three for almost ten years.) We aren't even sure exactly where the centre of that dot lies on the disk: our highest sounding rocket, the Nova-Orion block two, can barely rise two degrees above the plane of the disk before crashing back again. Here is the scope of our knowledge of our surroundings, derived from the continental-scale mapping cameras carried by Project Orion:

(A salmon pink area almost half an inch in diameter lights up around the red sand grain on the face of the single.)

Of course, cameras at an altitude of a hundred thousand miles can't look down on new continents and discern signs of Communist infiltration; at best they can listen for radio transmissions and perform spectroscopic analyses of the atmospheric gasses above distant lands, looking for gasses characteristic of industrial development such as chlorofluorocarbons and nitrogen oxides.

This leaves us vulnerable to unpleasant surprises. Our long term strategic analyses imply that we are almost certainly not alone on the disk. In addition to the Communists, we must consider the possibility that whoever build this monstrous structure—clearly one of the wonders of the universe—might also live here. We must contemplate their motives for bringing us to this place. And then there are the aboriginal cultures discovered on continents F-29 and F-364, both now placed under quarantine. If some land masses bear aboriginal inhabitants, we may speculate that they, too, have been transported to the disk in the same manner as ourselves, for some as-yet unknown purpose. It is possible that they are genuine stone-age dwellers—or that they are the survivors of advanced civilizations that did not survive the transition to this environment. What is the possibility that there exists on the disk one or more advanced alien civilizations that are larger and more powerful than our own? And would we recognize them as such if we saw them? How can we go about estimating the risk of our encountering hostile Little Green Men—now that other worlds are in range of even a well-equipped sailboat, much less the *Savannah*-class nuclear powered exploration ships? Astronomers Carl Sagan and Daniel Drake estimate the probability as high—so high, in fact, that they believe there are several such civilizations out there.

We are not alone. We can only speculate about why we might have been brought here by the abductors, but we can be certain that it is only a matter of time before we encounter an advanced alien civilization that may well be hostile to us. This briefing film will now continue with an overview of our strategic preparations for first contact, and the scenarios within which we envisage this contingency arising, with specific reference to the Soviet Union as an example of an unfriendly ideological superpower…

Tenure Track

After two weeks, Maddy is sure she's going mad.

She and Bob have been assigned a small prefabricated house (not much more than a shack, although it has electricity and running water) on the edge of town. He's been drafted into residential works, put to work erecting more buildings: and this is the nearest thing to a success they've had, because after a carefully-controlled protest his status has been corrected, from just another set of unskilled hands to trainee surveyor. A promotion of which he is terribly proud, evidently taking it as confirmation that they've made the right move by coming here.

Maddy, meanwhile, has a harder time finding work. The district hospital is fully staffed. They don't need her, won't need her until the next shipload of settlers arrive, unless she wants to pack up her bags and go tramping around isolated ranch settlements in the outback. In a year's time the governor has decreed they'll establish another town-scale settlement, inland near the mining encampments on the edge of the Hoover Desert. Then they'll need medics to staff the new hospital: but for now, she's a spare wheel. Because Maddy is a city girl by upbringing and disposition, and not inclined to take a job tramping around the outback if she can avoid it.

She spends the first week and then much of the second mooching around town, trying to find out what she can do. She's not the only young woman in this predicament. While there's officially no unemployment, and the colony's dirigiste administration finds plenty of hard work for idle hands, there's also a lack of openings for ambulance crew, or indeed much of anything else she can do. Career-wise it's like a trip into the 1950's. Young, female, and ambitious? Lots of occupations simply don't exist out here on the fringe, and many others are closed or inaccessible. Everywhere she looks she sees mothers shepherding implausibly large flocks of toddlers their guardians pinch-faced from worry and exhaustion. Bob wants kids, although Maddy's not ready for that yet. But the alternatives on offer are limited.

Eventually Maddy takes to going through the "help wanted" ads on the bulletin board outside city hall. Some of them are legit: and at least a few are downright peculiar. One catches her eye: field assistant wanted for biological research. *I wonder?* she thinks, and goes in search of a door to bang on.

When she finds the door—raw wood, just beginning to bleach in the strong colonial sunlight—and bangs on it, John Martin opens it and blinks quizzically into the light. "Hello?" he asks.

"You were advertising for a field assistant?" She stares at him. *He's the entomologist,* right? She remembers his hands on the telescope on the deck of the ship. The voyage itself is already taking on the false patina of romance in her memories, compared to the dusty present it has delivered her to.

"I was? Oh—yes, yes. Do come in." He backs into the house—another of these identikit shacks, *colonial, family, for the use of*—and offers her a seat in what used to be the living room. It's almost completely filled by a work table and a desk and a tall wooden chest of sample drawers. There's an odd, musty smell, like old cobwebs and leaky demijohns of formalin. John shuffles around his den, vaguely disordered by the unexpected shock of company. There's something touchingly cute about him, like the subjects of his studies, Maddy thinks. "Sorry about the mess, I don't get many visitors. So, um, do you have any relevant experience?"

She doesn't hesitate: "None whatsoever, but I'd like to learn." She leans forward. "I qualified as a paramedic before we left. At college I was studying biology, but I had to drop out midway through my second year: I was thinking about going to medical school later, but I guess that's not going to happen here. Anyway, the hospital here has no vacancies, so I need to find something else to do. What exactly does a field assistant get up to?"

"Get sore feet." He grins lopsidedly. "Did you do any lab time? Field work?" Maddy nods hesitantly so he drags her meager college experiences out of her before he continues. "I've got a whole continent to explore and only one set of hands: we're spread thin out here. Luckily NSF budgeted to hire me an assistant. The assistant's job is to be my Man Friday; to help me cart equipment about, take samples, help with basic lab work—*very* basic—and so on. Oh, and if they're interested in entomology, botany, or anything else remotely relevant that's a plus. There aren't many unemployed life sciences people around here, funnily enough: have you had any chemistry?"

"Some," Maddy says cautiously; "I'm no biochemist." She glances round the crowded office curiously. "What are you meant to be doing?"

He sighs. "A primary survey of an entire continent. Nobody, but nobody, even bothered looking into the local insect ecology here. There're virtually no vertebrates, birds, lizards, what have you—but back home there are more species of beetle than everything else put together, and this place is no different. Did you know nobody has even sampled the outback fifty miles inland of here? We're doing nothing but throw up shacks along the coastline and open-cast quarries a few miles inland. There could be *anything* in the interior, absolutely anything." When he gets excited he starts gesticulating, Maddy notices, waving his hands around enthusiastically. She nods and smiles, trying to encourage him.

"A lot of what I'm doing is the sort of thing they were doing in the eighteenth and nineteenth century. Take samples, draw them, log their habitat and dietary habits, see if I can figure out their life cycle, try and work out who's kissing-cousins with what. Build a family tree. Oh, I also need to do the same with the vegetation, you know? And they want me to keep close watch on the other disks around Lucifer. 'Keep an eye out for signs of sapience,' whatever that means: I figure there's a bunch of leftovers in the astronomical community who feel downright insulted that whoever built this disk and brought us here didn't land on the White House lawn and introduce themselves. I'd better tell you right now, there's enough work here to occupy an army of zoologists and botanists for a century; you can get started on a PhD right here and now if you want. I'm only here for five years, but my successor should be okay about taking on an experienced RA … the hard bit is going to be maintaining focus. Uh, I can sort you out a subsistence grant from the governor-general's discretionary fund and get NSF to reimburse him, but it won't be huge. Would twenty Truman dollars a week be enough?"

Maddy thinks for a moment. Truman dollars—the local scrip—aren't worth a whole lot, but there's not much to spend them on. And Rob's earning for both of them anyway. And a PhD …*that could be my ticket back to civilization, couldn't it?* "I guess so," she says, feeling a sense of vast relief: so there's something she's useful for besides raising the next generation, after all. She tries to set aside the visions of herself, distinguished and not too much older, gratefully accepting a professor's chair at an ivy league university. "When do I start?"

On the Beach

Misha's first impressions of the disturbingly familiar alien continent are of an oppressively humid heat, and the stench of decaying jellyfish.

The *Sergei Korolev* floats at anchor in the river estuary, a huge streamlined visitor from another world. Stubby fins stick out near the waterline, like a seaplane with clipped wings: gigantic Kuznetsov atomic turbines in pods ride on booms to either side of its high-ridged back, either side of the launch/recovery catapults for its parasite MiG fighter-bombers, aft of the broad curve of the ekranoplan's bridge. Near the waterline, a boat bay is open: a naval spetsnaz team is busy loading their kit into the landing craft that will ferry them to the small camp on the beach. Misha, who stands just above the waterline, turns away from the giant ground effect ship and watches his commander, who is staring inland with a faint expression of worry. "Those trees—awfully close, aren't they?" Gagarin says, with the carefully studied stupidity that saw him through the first dangerous years after his patron Khrushchev's fall.

"That is indeed what captain Kirov is taking care of," replies Gorodin, playing his role of foil to the colonel-general's sardonic humor. And indeed shadowy figures in olive-green battle dress are stalking in and out of the trees, carefully laying tripwires and screamers in an arc around the beachhead. He glances to the left, where a couple of sailors with assault rifles stand guard, eyes scanning the jungle. "I wouldn't worry unduly sir."

"I'll still be happier when the outer perimeter is secure. And when I've got a sane explanation of this for the comrade General Secretary." Gagarin's humor evaporates: he turns and walks along the beach, towards the large tent that's already gone up to provide shelter from the heat of noon. The bar of solid sunlight—what passes for sunlight here—is already at maximum length, glaring like a rod of white-hot steel that impales the disk. (Some of the more superstitious call it the axle of heaven. Part of Gorodin's job is to discourage such non-materialist backsliding.)

The tent awning is pegged back: inside it, Gagarin and Misha find Major Suvurov and Academician Borisovitch leaning over a map. Already the scientific film crew—a bunch of dubious civilians from the TASS agency—are busy in a corner, preparing cans for shooting. "Ah, Oleg, Mikhail." Gagarin summons up a professionally photogenic smile. "Getting anywhere?"

Borisovitch, a slight, stoop-shouldered type who looks more like a janitor than a world-famous scientist, shrugs. "We were just talking about going along to the archaeological site, General. Perhaps you'd like to come, too?"

Misha looks over his shoulder at the map: it's drawn in pencil, and there's an awful lot of white space on it, but what they've surveyed so far is disturbingly familiar in outline—familiar enough to have given them all a number of sleepless nights even before they came ashore. Someone has scribbled a dragon coiling in a particularly empty corner of the void.

"How large is the site?" asks Yuri.

"Don't know, sir." Major Suvurov grumps audibly, as if the lack of concrete intelligence on the alien ruins is a personal affront. "We haven't found the end of it yet. But it matches what we know already."

"The aerial survey—" Mikhail coughs, delicately. "If you'd let me have another flight I could tell you more, General. I believe it may be possible to define the city limits narrowly, but the trees make it hard to tell."

"I'd give you the flight if only I had the aviation fuel," Gagarin explains patiently. "A chopper can burn its own weight in fuel in a day of surveying, and we have to haul everything out here from Archangel. In fact, when we go home we're leaving most of our flight-ready aircraft behind, just so that on the next trip out we can carry more fuel."

"I understand." Mikhail doesn't look happy. "As Oleg Ivanovitch says, we don't know how far it reaches. But I think when you see the ruins you'll understand why we need to come back here. Nobody's found anything like this before."

"Old Capitalist Man." Misha smiles thinly. "I suppose."

"Presumably." Borisovitch shrugs. "Whatever, we need to bring archaeologists. And a mass spectroscope for carbon dating. And other stuff." His face wrinkles unhappily. "They were here back when we would still have been living in caves!"

"Except we weren't," Gagarin says under his breath. Misha pretends not to notice.

By the time they leave the tent, the marines have got the *Korolev's* two BRDMs ashore. The big balloon-tired armored cars sit on the beach like monstrous amphibians freshly emerged from some primeval sea. Gagarin and Gorodin sit in the back of the second vehicle with the academician and the film crew: the lead BRDM carries their spetsnaz escort team. They maintain a dignified silence as the convoy rumbles and squeaks across the beach, up the gently sloping hillside, and then down towards the valley with the ruins.

The armored cars stop and doors open. Everyone is relieved by the faint breeze that cracks the oven-heat of the interior. Gagarin walks over to the nearest ruin—remnants of a wall, waist-high—and stands, hands on hips, looking across the wasteland.

"Concrete," says Borisovitch, holding up a lump of crumbled not-stone from the foot of the wall for Yuri to see.

"Indeed." Gagarin nods. "Any idea what this was?"

"Not yet." The camera crew is already filming, heading down a broad boulevard between rows of crumbling foundations. "Only the concrete has survived, and it's mostly turned to limestone. This is *old.*"

"Hmm." The First Cosmonaut walks round the stump of wall and steps down to the foundation layer behind it, looking around with interest. "Interior column here, four walls—they're worn down, aren't they? This stuff that looks like a red stain. Rebar? Found any intact ones?"

"Again, not yet sir," says Borisovitch. "We haven't looked everywhere yet, but …"

"Indeed." Gagarin scratches his chin idly. "Am I imagining it or are the walls all lower on that side?" He points north, deeper into the sprawling maze of overgrown rubble.

"You're right sir. No theory for it, though."

"You don't say." Gagarin walks north from the five-sided building's ruin, looks around. "This was a road?"

"Once, sir. It was nine meters wide—there seems to have been derelict ground between the houses, if that's what they were, and the road itself. "

"Nine meters, you say." Gorodin and the academician hurry to follow him as he strikes off, up the road. "Interesting stonework here, don't you think, Misha?"

"Yessir. Interesting stonework."

Gagarin stops abruptly and kneels. "Why is it cracked like this? Hey, there's sand down there. And, um. Glass? Looks like it's melted. Ah, trinitite."

"Sir?"

Borisovitch leans forward. "That's odd."

"What is?" asks Misha, but before he gets a reply both Gagarin and the researcher are up again and off towards another building.

"Look. The north wall." Gagarin's found another chunk of wall, this one a worn stump that's more than a meter high: he looks unhappy.

"Sir? Are you alright?" Misha stares at him. Then he notices the academician is also silent, and looking deeply perturbed. "What's wrong?"

Gagarin extends a finger, points at the wall. "You can just see him if you look close enough. How long would it take to fade, Mikhail? How many years have we missed them by?"

The academician licks his lips: "At least two thousand years, sir. Concrete cures over time, but it takes a very long time indeed to turn all the way to limestone. and then there's the weathering process to take account of. But the surface erosion...yes, that could fix the image from the flash. Perhaps. I'd need to ask a few colleagues back home."

"What's wrong?" the political officer repeats, puzzled.

The first cosmonaut grins humorlessly. "Better get your Geiger counter, Misha, and see if the ruins are still hot. Looks like we're not the only people on the disk with a geopolitical problem..."

Been here before

Brundle has finally taken the time to pull Gregor aside and explain what's going on; Gregor is not amused.

"Sorry you walked into it cold," says Brundle. "But I figured it would be best for you to see for yourself." He speaks with a Midwestern twang, and a flatness of affect that his colleagues sometimes mistake for signs of an underlying psychopathology.

"See what, in particular?" Gregor asks sharply. "*What,* in particular?" Gregor tends to repeat himself, changing only the intonation, when he's disturbed. He's human enough to recognize it as a bad habit but still finds it difficult to suppress the reflex.

Brundle pauses on the footpath, looks around to make sure there's nobody within earshot. The Mall is nearly empty today, and only a humid breeze stirs the waters on the pool. "Tell me what you think."

Gregor thinks for a moment, then summons up his full command of the local language: it's good practice. "The boys in the big house are asking for a CAB. It means someone's pulled his head out of his ass for long enough to realize they've got worse things to worry about than being shafted by the Soviets. Something's happened to make them realize they need a policy for dealing with the abductors. This is against doctrine, we need to do something about it fast before they start asking the right questions. Something's shaken them up, something secret, some HUMINT source from the wrong side of the curtain, perhaps. Could it be that man Gordievsky? But they haven't quite figured out what being here means. Sagan—does his presence mean what I think it does?"

"Yes," Brundle says tersely.

"Oh dear." A reflex trips and Gregor takes off his spectacles and polishes them nervously on his tie before replacing them. "Is it just him, or does it go further?" He leaves the rest of the sentence unspoken by convention—*is it* just him *you think we'll have to silence?*

"Further." Brundle tends to talk out of the side of his mouth when he's agitated, and from his current expression Gregor figures he's really upset. "Sagan and his friends at Cornell have been using the Arecibo dish to listen to the neighbors. This wasn't anticipated. Now they're asking for permission to beam a signal at the nearest of the other disks. Straight up, more or less; 'talk to us.' Unfortunately Sagan is well-known, which is why he caught the attention of our nominal superiors. Meanwhile, the Soviets have found something that scared them. CIA didn't hear about it through the usual assets—they contacted the State Department via the embassy, they're *that* scared." Brundle pauses a moment. "Sagan and his buddies don't know about that, of course."

"Why has nobody shot them already?" Gregor asks coldly.

Brundle shrugs. "We pulled the plug on their funding just in time. If we shot them as well someone might notice. Everything could go nonlinear while we were trying to cover it up. You know the problem; this is a semi-open society, inadequately controlled. A bunch of astronomers get together on their own initiative—academic conference, whatever—and decide to spend a couple of thousand bucks of research grant money from NIST to establish communications with the nearest disk. How are we supposed to police that kind of thing?"

"Shut down all their radio telescopes. At gunpoint, if necessary, but I figure a power cut or a congressional committee would be just as effective as leverage."

"Perhaps, but we don't have the Soviets' resources to work with. Anyway, that's why I dragged Sagan in for the CAB. It's a Potemkin village, you understand, to convince everybody he contacted that something is being done, but we're going to have to figure out how to shut him up."

"Sagan is the leader of the 'talk-to-us, alien gods' crowd, I take it."

"Yes."

"Well." Gregor considers his next words carefully. "Assuming he's still clean and uncontaminated, we can turn him or we can ice him. If we're going to turn him we need to do it convincingly—full Tellerization—and we'll need to come up with a convincing rationale. Use him to evangelize the astronomical community into shutting up or haring off in the wrong direction. Like Heisenberg and the Nazi nuclear weapons program." He snaps his fingers. "Why don't we tell him the truth? At least, something close enough to it to confuse the issue completely?"

"Because he's a member of the Federation of American Scientists and he won't believe anything we tell him without independent confirmation," Brundle mutters through one side of his mouth. "That's the trouble with using a government agency as our cover story."

They walk in silence for a minute. "I think it would be very dangerous to underestimate him," says Gregor. "He could be a real asset to us, but uncontrolled he's very dangerous. If we can't silence him we may have to resort to physical violence. And with the number of colonies they've already seeded, we can't be sure of getting them all."

"Itemize the state of their understanding," Brundle says abruptly. "I want a reality check. I'll tell you what's new after you run down the checklist."

"Okay." Gregor thinks for a minute. "Let us see. What everyone knows is that between zero three fifteen and twelve seconds and thirteen seconds Zulu time, on October second, sixty two, all the clocks stopped, the satellites went away, the star map changed, nineteen airliners and forty six ships in transit ended up in terminal trouble, and they found themselves transferred from a globe in the Milky Way galaxy to a disk which we figure is somewhere in the lesser Magellanic cloud. Meanwhile the Milky Way galaxy—we *assume* that's what it is—has changed visibly. Lots of metal-depleted stars, signs of macroscopic cosmic engineering, that sort of thing. The public explanation is that the visitors froze time, skinned the earth, and plated it over the disk. Luckily they're still bickering over whether the explanation is Minsky's copying, uh, hypothesis, or that guy Moravec with his digital simulation theory."

"Indeed." Brundle kicks at a paving stone idly. "Now. What is your forward analysis?"

"Well, sooner or later they're going to turn dangerous. They have the historic predisposition towards teleological errors, to belief in a giant omnipotent creator and a *purpose* to their existence. If they start speculating about the intentions of a transcendent intelligence, it's likely they'll eventually ask whether their presence here is symptomatic of God's desire to probe the circumstances of its own birth. After all, we have evidence of how many technological species on the disk, ten million, twelve? Replicated many times, in some cases. They might put it together with their concept of manifest destiny and conclude that they are, in fact, doomed to give birth to God. Which is an entirely undesirable conclusion for them to reach from our point of view. Teleologists being bad neighbors, so to speak."

"Yes indeed," Brundle says thoughtfully, then titters quietly to himself for a moment.

"This isn't the first time they've avoided throwing around H-bombs in bulk. That's unusual for primate civilizations. If they keep doing it, they could be dangerous."

"Dangerous is relative," says Brundle. He titters again. Things move inside his mouth.

"Don't *do* that!" Gregor snaps. He glances round instinctively, but nothing happens.

"You're jumpy." Brundle frowns. "Stop worrying so much. We don't have much longer here."

"Are we being ordered to move? Or to prepare a sterilization strike?"

"Not yet." Brundle shrugs. "We have further research to continue with before a decision is reached. The Soviets have made a discovery. Their crewed exploration program. The *Korolev* lucked out."

"They—" Gregor tenses. "What did they find?" He knows about the big nuclear-powered Ekranoplan, the dragon of the Caspian, searching the seven oceans for new worlds to conquer. He even knows about the small fleet they're trying to build at Archangelsk, the ruinous expense of it. But this is new. "What did they *find?*"

Brundle grins humorlessly. "They found ruins. Then they spent another eight weeks mapping the coastline. They've confirmed what they found, they sent the State Department photographs, survey details—the lot." Brundle gestures at the Cuban War monument, the huge granite column dominating the Mall, its shadow pointing towards the Capitol. "They found Washington DC, in ruins. One hundred and forty thousand miles *that* way." He points due north. "They're not total idiots, and it's the first time they've found one of their own species-transfer cognates. They might be well on their way to understanding the truth, but luckily our comrades in Moscow have that side of the affair under control. But they communicated their discovery to the CIA before it could be suppressed, which raises certain headaches.

"We must make sure that nobody *here* asks *why*. So I want you to start by dealing with Sagan."

Collecting Jar

It's noon, and the rippling heat haze turns the horizon to fog in the distance. Maddy tries not to move too much: the cycads cast imperfect shadows, and she can feel the Venetian blinds of light burning into her pale skin. She sighs slightly as she hefts the heavy canvas sample bag out of the back of the Land Rover: John will be needing it soon, once he's finished photographing the mock-termite nests. It's their third field trip together, their furthest dash into the outback, and she's already getting used to working with John. He's surprisingly easy to get on with, because he's so absorbed in his work that he's refreshingly free of social expectations. If she didn't know better she could almost let her guard down and start thinking of him as a friend, not an employer.

The heat makes her mind drift: she tries to remember what sparked her most recent quarrel with Bob, but it seems so distant and irrelevant now—like home, like Bob arguing with her father, like their hurried registry-office wedding and furtive emigration board hearing. All that makes sense now is the stifling heat, the glare of not-sunlight, John working with his camera out in the noonday sun where only mad dogs and Englishmen dare go. Ah, *it was the washing*. Who was going to do the washing while Maddy was away on the two-day field trip? Bob seemed to think he was doing her a favor, cooking for himself and taking his clothes to the single over-used public laundry. (Some year real soon now they'd get washing machines, but not yet…) Bob seemed to think he was being big-hearted, not publicly getting jealous all over her having a job that took her away from home with a male superior who was notoriously single. Bob seemed to think he was some kind of progressive liberated man, for putting up with a wife who had read Betty Freidan and didn't shave her armpits. *Fuck you, Bob,* she thinks tiredly, and tugs the heavy strap of the sample case over her shoulder and turns to head in John's direction. There'll be time to sort things out with Bob later. For now, she's got a job to do.

John is leaning over the battered camera, peering through its viewfinder in search of…something. "What's up?" she asks.

"Mock termites are up," he says, very seriously. "See the entrances?" The mock termites are what they've come to take a look at—nobody's reported on them from close up, but they're very visible as soon as you venture into the dusty plain. She peers at the foot of the termite mound, a baked clay hump in the soil that seems to writhe with life. There are little pipe-like holes, tunnels almost, emerging from the base of the mound, and little black mock-termites dancing in and out of the holes in never-ending streams. *Little* is relative—they're almost as large as mice. "Don't touch them," he warns.

"Are they poisonous?" asks Maddy.

"Don't know, don't want to find out this far from the hospital. The fact that there are no vertebrates here—" he shrugs. "We know they're poisonous to other insectoida."

Maddy puts the sample case down. "But nobody's been bitten, or died, or anything."

"Not that we know of." He folds back the lid of the case and she shivers, abruptly cold, imagining bleached bones lying unburied in the long grass of the inland plain, where no humans will live for centuries to come. "It's essential to take care out here. We could be missing for days before anyone noticed, and a search party wouldn't necessarily find us, even with the journey plan we filed."

"Okay." She watches as he takes out an empty sample jar and a label and carefully notes down time and date, distance and direction from the milestone at the heart of Fort Eisenhower. *Thirty six miles.* They might as well be on another planet. "You're taking samples?"

He glances round: "of course." Then he reaches into the side pocket of the bag and removes a pair of heavy gloves, which he proceeds to put on, and a trowel. "If you could put the case down over there?"

Maddy glances inside the case as he kneels down by the mock termite mound. It's full of jars with blank labels, neatly segregated, impassable quarantine zones for improbable species. She looks round. John is busy with the mock-termite mound. He's neatly lopped the top off it: inside, the earth is a squirming mass of—things. Black things, white things like bits of string, and a pulp of half-decayed vegetable matter that smells damply of humus. He probes the mound delicately with the trowel, seeking something. "Look," he calls over his shoulder. "It's a queen!"

Maddy hurries over. "Really?" she asks. Following his gloved finger, she sees something the size of her left forearm, white and glistening. It twitches, expelling something round, and she feels her gorge rise. "Ugh!"

"It's just a happy mother," John says calmly. He lowers the trowel, works it in under the queen and lifts her—and a collection of hangers-on, courtiers and bodyguards alike—over the jar. He tips, he shakes, and he twists the lid into place. Maddy stares at the chaos within. What is it like to be a mock termite, suddenly snatched up and transplanted to a mockery of home? What's it like to see the sun in an electric light bulb, to go about your business, blindly pumping out eggs and eating and foraging for leaves, under the eyes of inscrutable collectors? She wonders if Bob would understand if she tried to tell him. John stands up and lowers the glass jar into the sample case, then freezes. "Ouch," he says, and pulls his left glove off.

"Ouch." He says it again, more slowly. "I missed a small one. Maddy, medical kit, please. Atropine and neostigmine."

She sees his eyes, pinprick pupils in the noonday glare, and dashes to the Land Rover. The medical kit, olive green with a red cross on a white circle, seems to mock her: she rushes it over to John, who is now sitting calmly on the ground next to the sample case. "What do you need?" she asks.

John tries to point, but his gloved hand is shaking wildly. He tries to pull it off, but the swollen muscles resist attempts to loosen the glove. "Atropine—" A white cylinder, with a red arrow on one side: she quickly reads the label, then pushes it hard against his thigh, feels something spring-loaded explode inside it. John stiffens, then tries to stand up, the automatic syringe still hanging from his leg. He staggers stiff-legged towards the Land Rover and slumps into the passenger seat.

"Wait!" she demands. Tries to feel his wrist: "how many of them bit you?"

His eyes roll. "Just one. Silly of me. No vertebrates." Then he leans back. "I'm going to try and hold on. Your first aid training."

Maddy gets the glove off, exposing fingers like angry red sausages: but she can't find the wound on his left hand, can't find anything to suck the poison out of. John's breathing is labored and he twitches: he needs the hospital but it's at least a four hour drive away and she can't look after him while she drives. So she puts another syringe load of atropine into his leg and waits with him for five minutes while he struggles for breath hoarsely, then follows up with adrenalin and anything else she can think of that's good for handling anaphylactic shock. "Get us back," he manages to wheeze at her between emphysemic gasps. "Samples too."

After she gets him into the load bed of the truck, she dashes over to the mock termite mound with the spare petrol can. She splashes the best part of a gallon of fuel over the heap, coughing with the stink: she caps the jerry can, drags it away from the mound, then strikes a match and throws it flickering at the disordered insect kingdom. There's a soft *whump* as the igniting gas sets the mound aflame: small shapes writhe and crisp beneath an empty blue sky pierced by the glaring pinprick of S Doradus.

Maddy doesn't stay to watch. She hauls the heavy sample case back to the Land Rover, loads it into the trunk alongside John, and scurries back towards town as fast as she can.

She's almost ten miles away before she remembers the camera, left staring in cyclopean isolation at the scorched remains of the dead colony.

Homeward Bound

The big ground effect ship rumbles softly as it cruises across the endless expanse of the Dzerzhinsky Ocean at nearly three hundred knots, homeward bound at last. Misha sits in his cubbyhole—as shipboard political officer he rates an office of his own—and sweats over his report with the aid of a glass of Polish pear schnapps. Radio can't punch through more than a few thousand miles of air directly, however powerful the transmitters; on earth they used to bounce signals off the ionosphere or the moon, but that doesn't work here—the other disks are too far away to use as relays. There's a chain of transceiver buoys marching out across the ocean at two thousand kilometer intervals, but the equipment is a pig to maintain, very expensive to build, and nobody is even joking about stringing undersea cables across a million kilometers of sea floor. Misha's problem is that the expedition, himself included, is effectively stranded back in the eighteenth century, without even the telegraph to tie civilization together—which is a pretty pickle to find yourself in when you're the bearer of news that will make the Politburo shit a brick. He desperately wants to be able to boost this up the ladder a bit, but instead it's going to be his name and his alone on the masthead.

"Bastards. Why couldn't they give us a signal rocket or two?"

He gulps back what's left of the schnapps and winds a fresh sandwich of paper and carbon into his top-secret-eyes-only typewriter.

"Because it would weigh too much, Misha," the captain says right behind his left shoulder, causing him to jump and bang his head on the overhead locker.

When Misha stops swearing and Gagarin stops chuckling, the Party man carefully turns his stack of typescript face down on the desk then politely gestures the captain into his office. "What can I do for you, boss? And what do you mean, they're too heavy?"

Gagarin shrugs. "We looked into it. Sure, we could put a tape recorder and a transmitter into an ICBM and shoot it up to twenty thousand kilometers. Trouble is, it'd fall down again in an hour or so. The fastest we could squirt the message, it would cost about ten rubles a character—more to the point, even a lightweight rocket would weigh as much as our entire payload. Maybe in ten years." He sits down. "How are you doing with that report?"

Misha sighs. "How am I going to explain to Brezhnev that the Americans aren't the only mad bastards with hydrogen bombs out here? That we've found the new world and the new world is just like the old world, except it glows in the dark? And the only communists we've found so far are termites with guns?" For a moment he looks haggard. "It's been nice knowing you, Yuri."

"Come on! It can't be that bad—" Gagarin's normally sunny disposition is clouded.

"*You* try and figure out how to break the news to them." After identifying the first set of ruins, they'd sent one of their MiGs out, loaded with camera pods and fuel: a thousand kilometers inland it had seen the same ominous story of nuclear annihilation visited on an alien civilization: ruins of airports, railroads, cities, factories. A familiar topography in unfamiliar form.

This was New York—once, thousands of years before a giant stamped the bottom of Manhattan island into the sea bed—and that was once Washington DC. Sure there'd been extra skyscrapers, but they'd hardly needed the subsequent coastal cruise to be sure that what they were looking at was the same continent as the old capitalist enemy, thousands of years and millions of kilometers beyond a nuclear war. "We're running away like a dog that's seen the devil ride out, hoping that he doesn't see us and follow us home for a new winter hat."

Gagarin frowns. "Excuse me?" He points to the bottle of pear schnapps.

"You are my guest." Misha pours the First Cosmonaut a glass then tops up his own. "It opens certain ideological conflicts, Yuri. And nobody wants to be the bearer of bad news."

"Ideological—such as?"

"Ah." Misha takes a mouthful. "Well, we have so far avoided nuclear annihilation and invasion by the forces of reactionary terror during the Great Patriotic War, but only by the skin of our teeth. Now, doctrine has it that any alien species advanced enough to travel in space is almost certain to have discovered socialism, if not true communism, no? And that the enemies of socialism wish to destroy socialism, and take its resources for themselves. But what we've seen here is evidence of a different sort. This *was* America. It follows that somewhere nearby there is a continent that *was* home to another Soviet Union—two thousand years ago. But this America has been wiped out, and our elder Soviet brethren are not in evidence and they have not colonized this other-America—what can this mean?"

Gagarin's brow wrinkled. "They're dead too? I mean, that the alternate-Americans wiped them out in an act of colonialist imperialist aggression but did not survive their treachery," he adds hastily.

Misha's lips quirk in something approaching a grin: "Better work on getting your terminology right first time before you see Brezhnev, comrade," he says. "Yes, you are correct on the facts, but there are matters of *interpretation* to consider. No colonial exploitation has occurred. So either the perpetrators were also wiped out, or perhaps...well, it opens up several very dangerous avenues of thought. Because if New Soviet Man isn't home hereabouts, it implies that something happened to them, doesn't it? Where are all the true Communists? If it turns out that they ran into hostile aliens, then...well, theory says that aliens should be good brother socialists. Theory and ten rubles will buy you a bottle of vodka on this one. Something is badly wrong with our understanding of the direction of history."

"I suppose there's no question that there's something we don't know about," Gagarin adds in the ensuing silence, almost as an afterthought.

"Yes. And that's a fig-leaf of uncertainty we can hide behind, I hope." Misha puts his glass down and stretches his arms behind his head, fingers interlaced until his knuckles crackle. "Before we left, our agents reported signals picked up in America from—damn, I should not be telling you this without authorization. Pretend I said nothing." His frown returns.

"You sound as if you're having dismal thoughts," Gagarin prods.

"I *am* having dismal thoughts, comrade colonel-general, very dismal thoughts indeed. We have been behaving as if this world we occupy is merely a new geopolitical game board, have we not? Secure in the knowledge that brother socialists from beyond the stars brought us here to save us from the folly of the imperialist aggressors, or that anyone else we meet will be either barbarians or good communists, we have fallen into the pattern of an earlier age—expanding in all directions, recognizing no limits, assuming our manifest destiny. But what if there are limits? Not a barbed wire fence or a line in the sand, but something more subtle. Why does history demand success of *us*? What we know is the right way for humans on a human world, with an industrial society, to live. But this is not a human world. And what if it's a world we're not destined to succeed? Or what if the very circumstances which gave rise to Marxism are themselves transient, in the broader scale? What if there is a—you'll pardon me—a materialist God? We know this is our own far future we are living in. *Why* would any power vast enough to build this disk bring us here?"

Gagarin shakes his head. "There are no limits, my friend," he says, a trifle condescendingly: "If there were, do you think we would have gotten this far?"

Misha thumps his desk angrily. "Why do you think they put us somewhere where your precious rockets don't work?" he demands. "Get up on high, one push of rocket exhaust and you could be halfway to anywhere! But down here we have to slog through the atmosphere. We can't get away! Does that sound like a gift from one friend to another?"

"The way you are thinking sounds paranoid to me," Gagarin insists. "I'm not saying you're wrong, mind you: only—could you be overwrought? Finding those bombed cities affected us all, I think."

Misha glances out of his airliner-sized porthole: "I fear there's more to it than that. We're not unique, comrade; we've been here before. *And we all died.* We're a fucking duplicate, Yuri Alexeyevich, there's a larger context to all this. And I'm scared by what the politburo will decide to do when they see the evidence. Or what the Americans will do..."

Last Supper

Returning to Manhattan is a comfort of sorts for Gregor, after the exposed plazas and paranoid open vistas of the capital. Unfortunately he won't be here for long—he is, after all, on an assignment from Brundle—but he'll take what comfort he can from the deep stone canyons, the teeming millions scurrying purposefully about at ground level. The Big Apple is a hive of activity, as always, teeming purposeful trails of information leading the busy workers about their tasks. Gregor's nostrils flare as he stands on the sidewalk on Lexington and East 100th. There's an Italian restaurant Brundle recommended when he gave Gregor his briefing papers. "Their spaghetti al' polpette is to die for," Brundle told him. That's probably true, but what's inarguable is that it's only a couple of blocks away from the offices of the Exobiology Annex to Cornell's New York Campus, where Sagan is head of department.

Gregor opens the door and glances around. A waiter makes eye contact. "Table for one?"

"Two. I'm meeting—ah." Gregor sees Sagan sitting in a booth at the back of the restaurant and waves hesitantly. "He's already here."

Gregor nods and smiles at Sagan as he sits down opposite the professor. The waiter drifts over and hands him a menu. "Have you ordered?"

"I just got here." Sagan smiles guardedly. "I'm not sure why you wanted this meeting, Mr., uh, Samsa, isn't it?" Clearly he thinks he gets the joke—a typical mistake for a brilliant man to make.

Gregor allows his lower lip to twitch. "Believe me, I'd rather it wasn't necessary," he says, entirely truthfully. "But the climate in DC isn't really conducive to clear thought or long-range planning—I mean, we operate under constraints established by the political process. We're given questions to answer, we're not encouraged to come up with new questions. So what I'd like to do is just have an open-ended informal chat about anything that you think is worth considering. About our situation, I mean. In case you can open up any avenues we ought to be investigating that aren't on the map right now."

Sagan leans forward. "That's all very well," he says agreeably, "but I'm a bit puzzled by the policy process itself. We haven't yet made contact with any nonhuman sapients. I thought your committee was supposed to be assessing our policy options for when contact finally occurs. It sounds to me as if you're telling me that we already have a policy, and you're looking to find out if it's actually a viable one. Is that right?"

Gregor stares at him. "I can neither confirm nor deny that," he says evenly. Which is the truth. "But if you want to take some guesses I can either discuss things or clam up when you get too close," he adds, the muscles around his eyes crinkling conspiratorially.

"Aha." Sagan grins back at him boyishly. "I get it." His smile vanishes abruptly. "Let me guess. The policy is predicated on MAD, isn't it?"

Gregor shrugs then glances sideways, warningly: the waiter is approaching. "I'll have a glass of the house red," he says, sending the fellow away as fast as possible. "Deterrence presupposes communication, don't you think?" Gregor asks.

"True." Sagan picks up his bread knife and absent-mindedly twirls it between finger and thumb. "But it's how the idiots—excuse me, our elected leaders—treat threats, and I can't see them responding to tool-using non-humans as anything else." He stares at Gregor. "Let me see if I've got this right. Your committee pulled me in because there has, in fact, been a contact between humans and non-human intelligences—or at least some sign that there are NHIs out there. The existing policy for dealing with it was drafted some time in the sixties under the influence of the hangover left by the Cuban war, and it basically makes the *conservative* assumption that any aliens are green-skinned Soviets and the only language they talk is nuclear annihilation. This policy is now seen to be every bit as bankrupt as it sounds but nobody knows what to replace it with because there's no data on the NHIs. Am I right?"

"I can neither confirm nor deny that," says Gregor.

Sagan sighs. "Okay, play it your way." He closes his menu. "Ready to order?"

"I believe so." Gregor looks at him. "The spaghetti al' polpette is really good here," he adds.

"Really?" Sagan smiles. "Then I'll try it."

They order, and Gregor waits for the waiter to depart before he continues. "Suppose there's an alien race out there. More than one. You know about the multiple copies of Earth. The uninhabited ones. We've been here before. Now let's see…suppose the aliens aren't like us. Some of them are recognizable, tribal primates who use tools made out of metal, sea-dwelling ensemble entities who communicate by ultrasound. But others—most of them—are social insects who use amazingly advanced biological engineering to grow what they need. There's some evidence that they've colonized some of the empty Earths. They're aggressive and territorial and they're so different that…well, for one thing we think they don't actually have conscious minds except when they need them. They control their own genetic code and build living organisms tailored to whatever tasks they want carrying out. There's no evidence that they want to talk to us, and some evidence that they may have emptied some of those empty Earths of their human population. And because of their, um, decentralized ecosystem and biological engineering, conventional policy solutions won't work. The military ones, I mean."

Gregor watches Sagan's face intently as he describes the scenario. There is a slight cooling of the exobiologist's cheeks as his peripheral arteries contract with shock: his pupils dilate and his respiration rate increases. Sour pheromones begin to diffuse from his sweat ducts and organs in Gregor's nasal sinuses respond to them.

"You're kidding?" Sagan half-asks. He sounds disappointed about something.

"I wish I was." Gregor generates a faint smile and exhales breath laden with oxytocin and other peptide messengers fine-tuned to human metabolism. In the kitchen, the temporary chef who is standing in for the regular one—off sick, due to a bout of food poisoning—will be preparing Sagan's dish. Humans are creatures of habit: once his meal arrives the astronomer will eat it, taking solace in good food. (Such a shame about the chef.) "They're not like us. SETI assumes that NHIs are conscious and welcome communication with humans and, in fact, that humans aren't atypical. But let's suppose that humans *are* atypical. The human species has only been around for about a third of a million years, and has only been making metal tools and building settlements for ten thousand. What if the default for sapient species is measured in the millions of years? And they develop strong defense mechanisms to prevent other species moving into their territory?"

"That's incredibly depressing," Sagan admits after a minute's contemplation. "I'm not sure I believe it without seeing some more evidence. That's why we wanted to use the Arecibo dish to send a message, you know. The other disks are far enough away that we're safe, whatever they send back: they can't possibly throw missiles at us, not with a surface escape velocity of twenty thousand miles per second, and if they send unpleasant messages we can stick our fingers in our ears."

The waiter arrives, and slides his entree in front of Sagan.

"Why do you say that?" asks Gregor.

"Well, for one thing, it doesn't explain the disk. We couldn't make anything like it—I suppose I was hoping we'd have some idea of who did? But from what you're telling me, insect hives with advanced biotechnology…that doesn't sound plausible."

"We have some information on that." Gregor smiles reassuringly. "For the time being, the important thing to recognize is that the species who are on the disk are roughly equivalent to ourselves in technological and scientific understanding. Give or take a couple of hundred years."

"Oh." Sagan perks up a bit.

"Yes," Gregor continues. "We have some information—I can't describe our sources—but anyway. You've seen the changes to the structure of the galaxy we remember. How would you characterize that?"

"Hmm." Sagan is busy with a mouthful of delicious tetrodotoxin-laced meatballs. "It's clearly a Kardashev type-III civilization, harnessing the energy of an entire galaxy. What else?"

Gregor smiles. "Ah, those Russians, obsessed with coal and steel production! This is the information age, Dr. Sagan. What would the informational resources of a galaxy look like, if they were put to use? And to what use would an unimaginably advanced civilization put them?"

Sagan looks blank for a moment, his fork pausing halfway to his mouth, laden with a deadly promise. "I don't see—ah!" He smiles, finishes his forkful, and nods. "Do I take it that we're living in a nature reserve? Or perhaps an archaeology experiment?"

Gregor shrugs. "Humans are time-binding animals," he explains. "So are all the other tool-using sentient species we have been able to characterize; it appears to be the one common factor, they like to understand their past as a guide to their future. We have sources that have…think of a game of Chinese whispers? The belief that is most widely held is that the disk was made by the agencies we see at work restructuring the galaxy, to house their, ah, experiments in ontology. To view their own deep past, before they became whatever they are, and to decide whether the path through which they emerged was inevitable or a low probability outcome. The reverse face of the Drake equation, if you like."

Sagan shivers. "Are you telling me we're just … memories? Echoes from the past, reconstituted and replayed some unimaginable time in the future? That this entire monstrous joke of a cosmological experiment is just a sideshow?"

"Yes, Dr. Sagan," Gregor says soothingly. "After all, the disk is not so large compared to an entire galaxy, don't you think? And I would not say the sideshow is unimportant. Do you ever think about your own childhood? And wonder whether the you that sits here in front of me today was the inevitable product of your upbringing? Or could you have become someone completely different—an airline pilot, for example, or a banker? Alternatively, could *someone else* have become *you*? What set of circumstances combine to produce an astronomer and exobiologist? Why should a God not harbour the same curiosity?"

"So you're saying it's introspection, with a purpose. The galactic civilization wants to see its own birth."

"The galactic hive mind," Gregor soothes, amused at how easy it is to deal with Sagan. "Remember, information is key. Why should human-level intelligences be the highest level?" All the while he continues to breathe oxytocin and other peptide neurotransmitters across the table towards Sagan. "Don't let such speculations ruin your meal," he adds, phrasing it as an observation rather than an implicit command.

Sagan nods and returns to using his utensils. "That's very thought-provoking," he says, as he gratefully raises the first mouthful to his lips. "If this is based on hard intelligence it…well, I'm worried. Even if it's inference, I have to do some thinking about this. I hadn't really been thinking along these lines."

"I'm sure if there's an alien menace we'll defeat it," Gregor assures him as he masticates and swallows the neurotoxin-laced meatball in tomato sauce. And just for the moment, he is content to relax in the luxury of truth: "Just leave everything to me and I'll see that your concerns are communicated to the right people. Then we'll do something about your dish and everything will work out for the best."

Poor prognosis

Maddy visits John regularly in hospital. At first it's a combination of natural compassion and edgy guilt; John is pretty much alone on this continent of lies, being both socially and occupationally isolated, and Maddy can convince herself that she's helping him feel in touch, motivating him to recover. Later on it's a necessity of work—she's keeping the lab going, even feeding the squirming white horror in the earth-filled glass jar, in John's absence—and partly boredom. It's not as if Bob's at home much. His work assignments frequently take him to new construction sites up and down the coast. When he is home they frequently argue into the small hours, picking at the scabs on their relationship with the sullen pinch-faced resentment of a couple fifty years gone in despair at the wrongness of their shared direction. So she escapes by visiting John and tells herself that she's doing it to keep his spirits up as he learns to use his prostheses.

"You shouldn't blame yourself," he tells her one afternoon when he notices her staring. "If you hadn't been around I'd be dead. Neither of us was to know."

"Well." Maddy winces as he sits up, then raises the tongs to his face to nudge the grippers apart before reaching for the water-glass. "That won't—" She changes direction in mid sentence—"make it easier to cope."

"We're all going to have to cope," he says gnomically, before relaxing back against the stack of pillows. He's a lot better now than he was when he first arrived, delirious with his hand swollen and blackening, but the after-effects of the mock termite venom have weakened him in other ways. "I want to know why those things don't live closer to the coast. I mean, if they did we'd never have bothered with the place. After the first landing, that is." He frowns. "If you can ask at the crown surveyor's office if there are any relevant records, that would help."

"The crown surveyor's not very helpful." That's an understatement. The crown surveyor is some kind of throwback; last time she went in to his office to ask about maps of the northeast plateau he'd asked her whether her husband approved of her running around like this. "Maybe when you're out of here." She moves her chair closer to the side of the bed.

"Doctor Smythe says next week, possibly Monday or Tuesday." John sounds frustrated. "The pins and needles are still there." It's not just his right hand, lopped off below the elbow and replaced with a crude affair of padding and spring steel; the venom spread and some of his toes had to be amputated. He was fitting when Maddy reached the hospital, four hours after he was bitten. She knows she saved his life, that if he'd gone out alone he'd almost certainly have been killed, so why does she feel so bad about it?

"You're getting better," Maddy insists, covering his left hand with her own. "You'll see." She smiles encouragingly.

"I wish—" For a moment John looks at her; then he shakes his head minutely and sighs. He grips her hand with his fingers. They feel weak, and she can feel them trembling with the effort. "Leave Johnson—" the surveyor—"to me. I need to prepare an urgent report on the mock termites before anyone else goes poking them."

"How much of a problem do you think they're going to be?"

"Deadly." He closes his eyes for a few seconds, then opens them again. "We've got to map their population distribution. And tell the governor-general's office. I counted twelve of them in roughly an acre, but that was a rough sample and you can't extrapolate from it.

We also need to learn whether they've got any unusual swarming behaviors—like army ants, for example, or bees. Then we can start investigating whether any of our insecticides work on them. If the governor wants to start spinning out satellite towns next year, he's going to need to know what to expect. Otherwise people are going to get hurt." *Or killed,* Maddy adds silently.

John is very lucky to be alive: Doctor Smythe compared his condition to a patient he'd once seen who'd been bitten by a rattler, and that was the result of a single bite by a small one. *If the continental interior is full of the things, what are we going to do?* Maddy wonders.

"Have you seen any sign of her majesty feeding?" John asks, breaking into her train of thought.

Maddy shivers. "Turtle tree leaves go down well," she says quietly. "And she's given birth to two workers since we've had her. They chew the leaves to mulch then regurgitate it for her."

"Oh, really? Do they deliver straight into her mandibles?"

Maddy squeezes her eyes tight. This is the bit she was really hoping John wouldn't ask her about. "No," she says faintly.

"Really?" He sounds curious.

"I think you'd better see for yourself." Because there's no way in hell that Maddy is going to tell him about the crude wooden spoons the mock termite workers have been crafting from the turtle tree branches, or the feeding ritual, and what they did to the bumbler fly that got into the mock termite pen through the chicken wire screen.

He'll just have to see for himself.

Rushmore

The *Korolev* is huge for a flying machine but pretty small in nautical terms. Yuri is mostly happy about this. He's a fighter jock at heart and he can't stand Navy bullshit. Still, it's a far cry from the MiG-17s he qualified in. It doesn't have a cockpit, or even a flight deck—it has a *bridge,* like a ship, with the pilots, flight engineers, navigators, and observers sitting in a horseshoe around the captain's chair. When it's thumping across the sea barely ten meters above the wave-tops at nearly five hundred kilometers per hour, it rattles and shakes until the crew's vision blurs. The big reactor-powered turbines in the tail pods roar and the neutron detectors on the turquoise radiation bulkhead behind them tick like demented death-watch beetles: the rest of the crew are huddled down below in the nose, with as much shielding between them and the engine rooms as possible. It's a white-knuckle ride, and Yuri has difficulty resisting the urge to curl his hands into fists because whenever he loses concentration his gut instincts are telling him to grab the stick and pull up. The ocean is no aviator's friend, and skimming across this infinite gray expanse between planet-sized land-masses forces Gagarin to confront the fact that he is not, by instinct, a sailor.

They're two days outbound from the new-old North America, forty thousand kilometers closer to home and still weeks away even though they're cutting the corner on their parabolic exploration track. The fatigue is getting to him as he takes his seat next to Misha—who is visibly wilting from his twelve hour shift at the con—and straps himself in. "Anything to report?" He asks.

"I don't like the look of the ocean ahead," says Misha. He nods at the navigation station to Gagarin's left: Shaw, the Irish ensign, sees him and salutes.

"Permission to report, sir?" Gagarin nods. "We're coming up on a thermocline boundary suggestive of another radiator wall, this time surrounding uncharted seas. Dead reckoning says we're on course for home but we haven't charted this route and the surface waters are getting much cooler. Any time now we should be spotting the radiators, and then we're going to have to start keeping a weather eye out."

Gagarin sighs: exploring new uncharted oceans seemed almost romantic at first, but now it's a dangerous but routine task. "You have kept the towed array at altitude?" he asks.

"Yes sir," Misha responds. The towed array is basically a kite-born radar, tugged along behind the *Korolev* on the end of a kilometer of steel cable to give them some warning of obstacles ahead. "Nothing showing—"

Right on cue, one of the radar operators raises a hand and waves three fingers.

"—Correction, radiators ahoy, range three hundred, bearing ...okay, let's see it."

"Maintain course," Gagarin announces. "Let's throttle back to two hundred once we clear the radiators, until we know what we're running into." He leans over to his left, watching over Shaw's shoulder.

The next hour is unpleasantly interesting. As they near the radiator fins, the water and the air above it cool down. The denser air helps the *Korolev* generate lift, which is good, but they need it, which is bad. The sky turns gray and murky and rain falls in continuous sheets that hammer across the armored bridge windows like machine gun fire. The ride becomes gusty as well as bumpy, until Gagarin orders two of the nose turbines started just in case they hit a down-draft. The big jet engines guzzle fuel and are usually shut down in cruise flight, used only for take-off runs and extraordinary situations. But punching through a cold front and a winter storm isn't flying as usual as far as Gagarin's concerned, and the one nightmare all Ekranoplan drivers face is running into a monster ocean wave nose-first at cruise speed.

Presently the navigators identify a path between two radiator fins, and Gagarin authorizes it. He's beginning to relax as the huge monoliths loom out of the gray clouds ahead when one of the sharp-eyed pilots shouts: "Icebergs!"

"*Fucking* hell." Gagarin sits bolt upright. "Start all boost engines! Bring up full power on both reactors! Lower flaps to nine degrees and get us the hell out of this!" He turns to Shaw, his face gray. "Bring the towed array aboard, *now.*"

"Shit." Misha starts flipping switches on his console, which doubles as damage control central. *"Icebergs?"*

The huge ground-effect ship lurches and roars as the third pilot starts bleeding hot exhaust gasses from the running turbines to start the other twelve engines. They've probably got less than six hours' fuel left, and it takes fifteen minutes on all engines to get off the water, but Gagarin's not going to risk meeting an iceberg head-on in ground-effect. The Ekranoplan can function as a huge, lumbering, ungainly sea-plane if it has to; but it doesn't have the engine power to do so on reactors alone, or to leap-frog floating mountains of ice. And hitting an iceberg isn't on Gagarin's to-do list.

The rain sluices across the roof of the bridge and now the sky is louring and dark, the huge walls of the radiator slabs bulking in twilight to either side. The rain is freezing, supercooled droplets that smear the Korolev's wings with a lethal sheen of ice. "Where are the leading edge heaters?" Gagarin asks. "Come on!"

"Working, sir," calls the number four pilot. Moments later the treacherous rain turns to hail stones, rattling and booming but fundamentally unlikely to stick to the flight surfaces and build up weight until it flips the ship over. "I think we're going to—"

A white and ghostly wall comes into view in the distance, hammering towards the bridge windows like a runaway freight train. Gagarin's stomach lurches. "Pull up, pull up!" The first and second pilots are struggling with the hydraulically boosted controls as the *Korolev's* nose pitches up almost ten degrees, right out of ground effect. "Come on!"

They make it.

The iceberg slams out of the darkness of the storm and the sea like the edge of the world; fifty meters high and as massive as mountains, it has lodged against the aperture between the radiator fins. Billions of tons of pack-ice has stopped dead in the water, creaking and groaning with the strain as it butts up against the infinite. The *Korolev* skids over the leading edge of the iceberg, her keel barely clearing it by ten meters, and continues to climb laboriously into the darkening sky. The blazing eyes of her reactors burn slick scars into the ice below. Then they're into the open water beyond the radiator fins, and although the sea below them is an expanse of whiteness they are also clear of icy mountains.

"Shut down engines three through fourteen," Gagarin orders once he regains enough control to keep the shakes out of his voice. "Take us back down to thirty meters, lieutenant. Meteorology, what's our situation like?"

"Arctic or worse, comrade general." The meteorologist, a hatchet-faced woman from Minsk, shakes her head. "Air temperature outside is thirty below, pressure is high." The rain and hail has vanished along with the radiators and the clear seas—and the light, for it is now fading towards nightfall.

"Hah. Misha, what do you think?"

"I think we've found our way into the freezer, sir. Permission to put the towed array back up?"

Gagarin squints into the darkness. "Lieutenant, keep us at two hundred steady. Misha, yes, get the towed array back out again. We need to see where we're going."

The next three hours are simultaneously boring and fraught. It's darker and colder than a Moscow apartment in winter during a power cut; the sea below is ice from horizon to horizon, cracking and groaning and splintering in a vast expanding V-shape behind the *Korolev's* pressure wake. The spectral ruins of the Milky Way galaxy stretch overhead, reddened and stirred by alien influences. Misha supervises the relaunch of the towed array, then hands over to Major Suvurov before stiffly standing and going below to the unquiet bunk room. Gagarin sticks to a quarter-hourly routine of reports, making sure that he knows what everyone is doing. Bridge crew come and go for their regular station changes. It is routine, and deadly with it. Then:

"Sir, I have a return. Permission to report?"

"Go ahead." Gagarin nods to the navigator. "Where?"

"Bearing zero—it's horizon to horizon—there's a crest rising up to ten meters above the surface. Looks like landfall, range one sixty and closing. Uh, there's a gap and a more distant landfall at thirty-five degrees, peak rising to two hundred meters."

"That's some cliff." Gagarin frowns. He feels drained, his brain hazy with the effort of making continual decisions after six hours in the hot seat and more than two days of this thumping roaring progression. He glances round. "Major? Please summon Colonel Gorodin. Helm, come about to zero thirty five. We'll take a look at the gap and see if it's a natural inlet. If this is a continental mass we might as well take a look before we press on for home."

For the next hour they drive onwards into the night, bleeding off speed and painting in the gaps in the radar map of the coastline. It's a bleak frontier, inhumanly cold, with a high interior plateau. There are indeed two headlands, promontories jutting into the coast from either side of a broad, deep bay. Hills rise from one of the promontories and across the bay. Something about it strikes Gagarin as strangely familiar, if only he could place it. Another echo of Earth? But it's too cold by far, a deep Antarctic chill. And he's not familiar with the coastline of Zemlya, the myriad inlets off the northeast passage, where the submarines cruise on eternal vigilant patrols to defend the frontier of the Rodina.

A thin predawn light stains the icy hilltops gray as the *Korolev* cruises slowly between the headlands—several kilometers apart—and into the wide open bay beyond. Gagarin raises his binoculars and scans the distant coastline. There are structures, straight lines! "Another ruined civilization?" He asks quietly.

"Maybe, sir. Think anyone could survive in this weather?" The temperature has dropped another ten degrees in the predawn chill, although the Ekranoplan is kept warm by the outflow of its two Kuznetsov aviation reactors.

"Hah."

Gagarin begins to sweep the northern coast when Major Suvurov stands up. "Sir! Over there!"

"Where?" Gagarin glances at him. Suvurov is quivering with anger, or shock, or something else. He, too, has his binoculars out.

"Over there! On the southern hillside."

"Where—" He brings his binoculars to bear as the dawn light spills across the shattered stump of an immense skyscraper.

There is a hillside behind it, a jagged rift where the land has risen up a hundred meters. It reeks of antiquity, emphasized by the carvings in the headland. Here is what the expedition has been looking for all along, the evidence that they are not alone.

"My God." Misha swears, shocked into politically incorrect language.

"Marx," says Gagarin, studying the craggy features of the nearest head. "I've seen this before, this sort of thing. The Americans have a memorial like it. Mount Rushmore, they call it."

"Don't you mean Easter Island?" asks Misha. "Sculptures left by a vanished people..."

"Nonsense! Look there, isn't that Lenin? And Stalin, of course." Even though the famous moustache is cracked and half of it has fallen away from the cliff. "But who's that next to them?"

Gagarin brings his binoculars to focus on the fourth head. Somehow it looks far less weathered than the others, as if added as an afterthought, perhaps some kind of insane statement about the mental health of its vanished builders. Both antennae have long

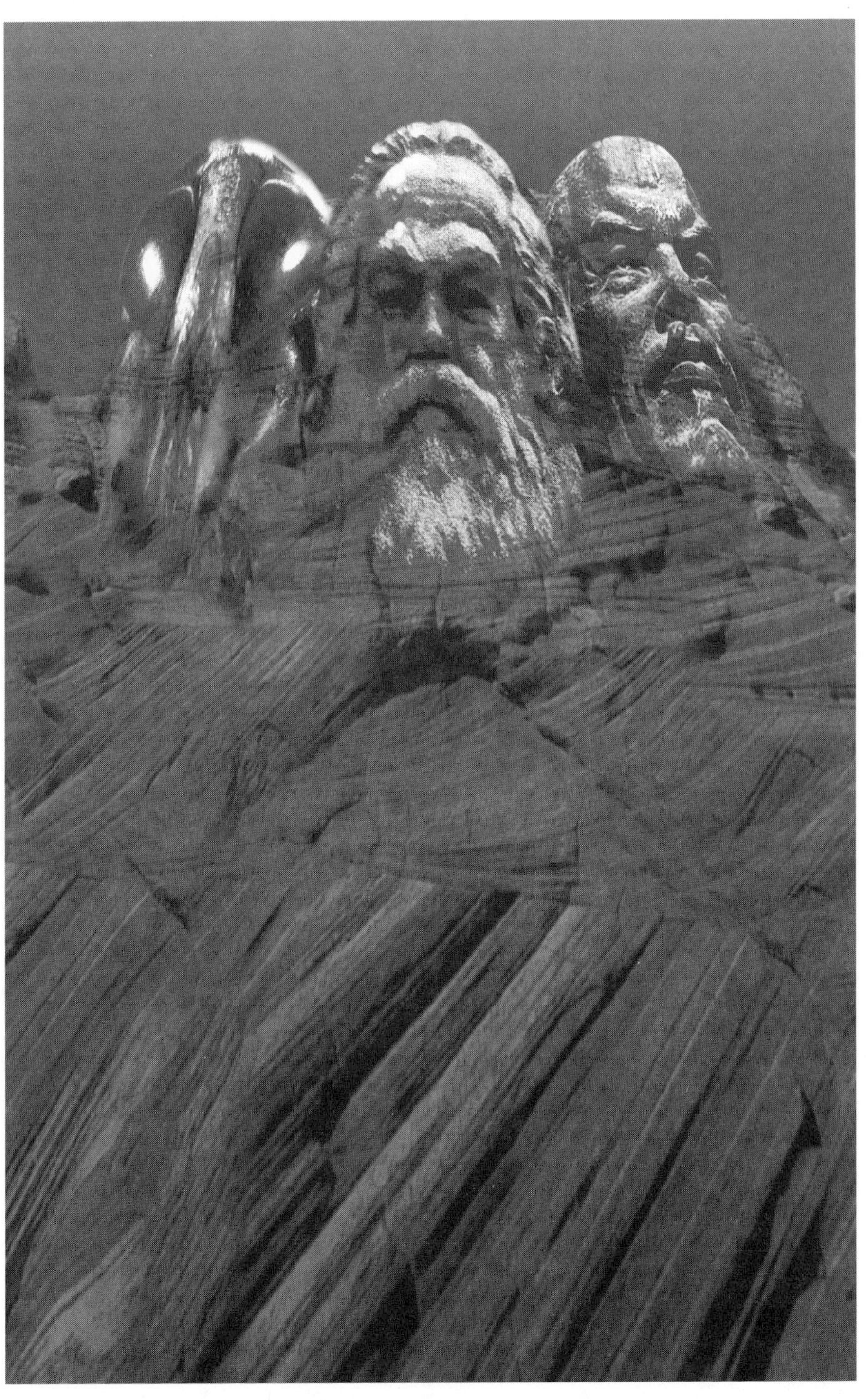

since broken off, and one of the mandibles is damaged, but the eyeless face is still recognizably unhuman. The insectile head stares eyelessly out across the frozen ocean, an enigma on the edge of a devastated island continent. "I think we've found the brother socialists," he mutters to Misha, his voice pitched low so that it won't carry over the background noise on the flight deck. "And you know what? Something tells me we didn't want to."

Anthropic error

As the summer dry season grinds on, Maddy finds herself spending more time at John's home-cum-laboratory, doing the cleaning and cooking for herself in addition to maintaining the lab books and feeding the live specimens. During her afternoons visiting in the hospital she helps him write up his reports. Losing his right hand has hit John hard: he's teaching himself to write again but his handwriting is slow and childish.

She finds putting in extra hours at the lab preferable to the empty and uncomfortable silences back in the two bedroom prefab she shares with Bob. Bob is away on field trips to outlying ranches and quarries half the time and working late the other half. At least, he says he's working late. Maddy has her suspicions. He gets angry if she isn't around to cook, and she gets angry right back at him when he expects her to clean, and they've stopped having sex. Their relationship is in fact going downhill rapidly, drying up and withering away in the arid continental heat, until going to work in John's living room among the cages and glass vivaria and books feels like taking refuge. She took to spending more time there, working late for real, and when Bob is away she sleeps on the wicker settee in the dining room.

One day, more than a month later than expected, Doctor Smythe finally decides that John is well enough to go home.

Embarrassingly, she's not there on the afternoon when he's finally discharged. Instead, she's in the living room, typing up a report on a sub-species of the turtle tree and its known parasites, when the screen door bangs and the front door opens. "Maddy?"

She squeaks before she can stop herself. "John?" She's out of the chair to help him with the battered suitcase the cabbie half-helpfully left on the front stoop.

"Maddy." He smiles tiredly. "I've missed being home."

"Come on in." She closes the screen door and carries the suitcase over to the stairs. He's painfully thin now, a far cry from the slightly too plump entomologist she'd met on the colony liner. "I've got lots of stuff for you to read—but not until you're stronger. I don't want you overworking and putting yourself back in hospital!"

"You're an angel." He stands uncertainly in his own living room, looking around as if he hadn't quite expected to see it again. "I'm looking forward to seeing the termites."

She shivers abruptly. "I'm not. Come on." She climbs the stairs with the suitcase, not looking back. She pushes through the door into the one bedroom that's habitable—he's been using the other one to store samples—and dumps the case on the rough dressing table. She's been up here before, first to collect his clothing while he was in hospital and later to clean and make sure there are no poisonous spiders lurking in the corners. It smells of camphor and dusty memories. She turns to face him. "Welcome home." She smiles experimentally.

He looks around. "You've been cleaning."

"Not much." She feels her face heat.

He shakes his head. "Thank you."

She can't decide what to say. "No, no, it's not like that. If I wasn't here I'd be..."

John shuffles. She blinks at him, feeling stupid and foolish. "Do you have room for a lodger?" She asks.

He looks at her and she can't maintain eye contact. It's all going wrong, not what she wanted.

“Things going badly?” he asks, cocking his head on one side and staring at her. “Forgive me, I don’t mean to pry—”

“No, no, it’s quite alright.” She sniffs. Takes a breath. “This continent breaks things. Bob hasn’t been the same since we arrived, or I, I haven’t. I need to put some space between us, for a bit.”

“Oh.”

“Oh.” She’s silent for a while. “I can pay rent—”

This is an excuse, a transparent rationalization, and not entirely true, but she’s saved from digging herself deeper into a lie because John manages to stumble and reaches out to steady himself with his right arm, which is still not entirely healed, and Maddy finds herself with his weight on her shoulder as he hisses in pain. “Ow! Ow!”

“I’m sorry! I’m sorry!”

“It wasn’t you—” They make it to the bed and she sits him down beside her. “I nearly blacked out then. I feel useless. I’m not half the man I was.”

“I don’t know about that,” she says absently, not quite registering his meaning. She strokes his cheek, feeling it slick with sweat. The pulse in his neck is strong. “You’re still recovering. I think they sent you home too early. Let’s get you into bed and rest up for a couple of hours, then see about something to eat. What do you say to that?”

“I shouldn’t need nursing,” he protests faintly as she bends down and unties his shoe-laces. “I don’t need…nursing.” He runs his fingers through her hair.

“This isn’t about nursing.”

Two hours later, the patient is drifting on the edge of sleep, clearly tired out by his physical therapy and the strain of homecoming. Maddy lies curled up against his shoulder, staring at the ceiling. She feels calm and at peace for the first time since she arrived here. *It’s not about Bob any more, is it?* She asks herself. *It’s not about what anybody expects of me. It’s about what I want, about finding my place in the universe.* She feels her face relaxing into a smile. Truly, for a moment, it feels as if the entire universe is revolving around her in stately synchrony.

John snuffles slightly then startles and tenses. She can tell he's come to wakefulness. "Funny," he says quietly, then clears his throat.

"What is?" *Please don't spoil this,* she prays.

"I wasn't expecting this." He moves beside her. "Wasn't expecting much of anything."

"Was it good?" She tenses.

"Do you still want to stay?" he asks hesitantly. "Damn, I didn't mean to sound as if—"

"No, I don't mind—" She rolls towards him, then is brought up short by a quiet, insistent tapping that travels up through the inner wall of the house. "Damn," she says quietly.

"What's that?" He begins to sit up.

"It's the termites."

John listens intently. The tapping continues erratically, on-again, off-again, bursts of clattering noise. "What is she doing?"

"They do it about twice a day," Maddy confesses. "I put her in the number two aquarium with a load of soil and leaves and a mesh lid on top. When they start making a racket I feed them."

He looks surprised. "This I've got to see."

The walls are coming back up again. Maddy stifles a sigh: it's not about her any more, it's about the goddamn mock termites. Anyone would think they were the center of the universe and she was just here to feed them. "Let's go look, then." John is already standing up, trying to pick up his discarded shirt with his prosthesis. "Don't bother," she tells him. "Who's going to notice, the insects?"

"I thought—" he glances at her, taken aback—"sorry, forget it."

She pads downstairs, pausing momentarily to make sure he's following her safely. The tapping continues, startlingly loud. She opens the door to the utility room in the back and turns on the light. "Look," she says.

The big glass-walled aquarium sits on the worktop. It's lined with rough-tamped earth and on top, there are piles of denuded branches and wood shavings. It's near dusk, and by the light filtering through the windows she can see mock-termites moving across the surface of the muddy dome that bulges above the queen's chamber. A group of them have gathered around a curiously straight branch: as she watches, they throw it against the glass like a battering ram against a castle wall. A pause, then they pick it up and pull back, and throw it again. They're huge for insects, almost two inches long: much bigger than the ones thronging the mounds in the outback. "That's odd." Maddy peers at them. "They've grown since yesterday."

"They? Hang on, did you take workers, or…?"

"No, just the queen. None of these bugs are more than a month old."

The termites have stopped banging on the glass. They form two rows on either side of the stick, pointing their heads up at the huge, monadic mammals beyond the alien barrier. Looking at them closely Maddy notices other signs of morphological change: the increasing complexity of their digits, the bulges at the back of their heads. *Is the queen's changing, too?* She asks herself, briefly troubled by visions of a malignant intelligence rapidly swelling beneath the surface of the vivarium, plotting its escape by moonlight.

John stands behind Maddy and folds his arms around her. She shivers. "I feel as if they're *watching* us."

"But to them it's not about us, is it?" He whispers in her ear. "Come on. All that's happening is you've trained them to ring a bell so the experimenters give them a snack. They think the universe was made for their convenience. Dumb insects, just a bundle of reflexes really. Let's feed them and go back to bed."

The two humans leave and climb the stairs together, arm in arm, leaving the angry aboriginal hive to plot its escape unnoticed.

It's always October the First

Gregor sits on a bench on the Esplanade, looking out across the river towards the Statue of Liberty. He's got a bag of stale bread crumbs and he's ministering to the flock of pigeons that scuttle and peck around his feet. The time is six minutes to three on the afternoon of October the First, and the year is irrelevant. In fact, it's too late. This is how it always ends, although the onshore breeze and the sunlight are unexpected bonus payments.

The pigeons jostle and chase one another as he drops another piece of crust on the pavement. For once he hasn't bothered to soak them overnight in 5% warfarin solution. There *is* such a thing as a free lunch, if you're a pigeon in the wrong place at the wrong time. He's going to be dead soon, and if any of the pigeons survive they're welcome to the wreckage.

There aren't many people about, so when the puffing middle aged guy in the suit comes into view, jogging along as if he's chasing his stolen wallet, Gregor spots him instantly. It's Brundle, looking slightly pathetic when removed from his man-hive. Gregor waves hesitantly, and Brundle alters course.

"Running late," he pants, kicking at the pigeons until they flap away to make space for him at the other end of the bench.

"Really?"

Brundle nods. "They should be coming over the horizon in another five minutes."

"How did you engineer it?" Gregor isn't particularly interested but technical chit-chat serves to pass the remaining seconds.

"Man-in-the-middle, ramified by all their intelligence assessments." Brundle looks self-satisfied. "Understanding their caste specialization makes it easier. Two weeks ago we told the GRU that MacNamara was using the NP-101 program as cover for a pre-emptive D-SLAM strike. At the same time we got the NOAA to increase their mapping launch frequency, and pointed the increased level of Soviet activity out to our sources in SAC. It doesn't take much to get the human hives buzzing with positive feedback."

Of course, Brundle and Gregor aren't using words for this incriminating exchange. Their phenotypically human bodies conceal some useful modifications, knobby encapsulated tumors of neuroectoderm that shield the delicate tissues of their designers, neural circuits that have capabilities human geneticists haven't even imagined. A visitor from a more advanced human society might start excitedly chattering about wet-phase nanomachines and neural-directed broadband packet radio, but nobody in New York on a sunny day in 1979 plus one million is thinking in those terms. They still think the universe belongs to their own kind, skull-locked social—but not eusocial—primates. Brundle and Gregor know better. They're workers of a higher order, carefully tailored to the task in hand, and although they *look* human there's less to their humanity than meets the eye. Even Gagarin can probably guess better, an individualist trapped in the machinery of a utopian political hive. The termites of New Iowa and a host of other Galapagos continents on the disk are not the future, but they're a superior approximation to anything humans have achieved, even those planetary instantiations that have doctored their own genome in order to successfully implement true eusocial societies. Group minds aren't prone to anthropic errors.

"So it's over, is it?" Gregor asks aloud, in the stilted serial speech to which humans are constrained.

"Yep. Any minute now—"

The air raid sirens begin to wail. Pigeons spook, exploding outward in a cloud of white panic.

"Oh, look."

The entity behind Gregor's eyes stares out across the river, marking time while his cancers call home. He's always vague about these last hours before the end of a mission—a destructive time, in which information is lost—but at least he remembers the rest. As do the hyphae of the huge rhizome network spreading deep beneath the park, thinking slow vegetable thoughts and relaying his sparky monadic flashes back to his mother by way of the engineered fungal strands that thread the deep ocean floors. The next version of him will be created knowing almost everything: the struggle to contain the annoying, hard-to-domesticate primates with their insistent paranoid individualism, the dismay of having to carefully sterilize the few enlightened ones like Sagan…

Humans are not useful. The future belongs to ensemble intelligences, hive minds. Even the mock-termite aboriginals have more to contribute. And Gregor, with his teratomas and his shortage of limbs, has more to contribute than most. The culture that sent him, and a million other anthropomorphic infiltrators, understands this well: he will be rewarded and propagated, his genome and memeome preserved by the collective even as it systematically eliminates yet another outbreak of humanity. The collective is well on its way towards occupying a tenth of the disk, or at least of sweeping it clean of competing life forms. Eventually it will open negotiations with its neighbors on the other disks, joining the process of forming a distributed consciousness that is a primitive echo of the vast ramified intelligence wheeling across the sky so far away. And this time round, knowing *why* it is being birthed, the new God will have a level of self-understanding denied to its parent.

Gregor anticipates being one of the overmind's memories: it is a fate none of these humans will know save at second-hand, filtered through his eusocial sensibilities. To the extent that he bothers to consider the subject, he thinks it is a disappointment. He may be here to help exterminate them, but it's not a personal grudge: it's more like pouring gasoline on a troublesome ant heap that's settled in the wrong back yard. The necessity irritates him, and he grumbles aloud in Brundle's direction: "If they realized how thoroughly they'd been infiltrated, or how badly their own individuality lets them down—"

Flashes far out over the ocean, ruby glare reflected from the thin tatters of stratospheric cloud.

"—They might learn to cooperate some day. Like us."

More flashes, moving closer now as the nuclear battlefront evolves.

Brundle nods. "But then, they wouldn't be human any more. And in any case, they're much too late. A million years too late."

A flicker too bright to see, propagating faster than the signaling speed of nerves, punctuates their conversation. Seconds later, the mach wave flushes their cinders from the bleached concrete of the bench. Far out across the disk, the game of ape and ant continues; but in this place and for the present time, the question has been answered. And there are no human winners.